Ninja Kids

Book 7

The Ninja Chronicles – Part One

By Adam Oakley

COPYRIGHT

ISBN: 978-1-912720-72-9

www.InnerPeaceNow.com

www.AdamOakleyBooks.com

Published by Oakhouse Publications.

Oakhouse Publications

Contents

Welcome

Nunchuks

Throwing Darts

若
武
者

Throwing Stars

Daggers

Young Warrior

Ninja Swords

Chapter 1 - The Ninja Chronicles

When Myasako was resting at home, weeks after the battle for the Shinwa Forest had ended, he heard his father moving around in the room beside him. It sounded as if he was shifting things around, lifting things up and opening doors.

Myasako stood at the doorway of the room, and his father had his back to him.

"I knew it was still here, somewhere," Kuyasaki said. "My master said he would keep it hidden until the time was right. And now the time must be right. These are The Ninja Chronicles."

Kuyasaki turned and handed Myasako an old, dusty book with a picture of a ninja on the front. But the ninja was not dressed in black. It was dressed in grey, baggy clothes.

"That was the Lightning Ninja," Kuyasaki said. "These are the tales of ninjas who lived before us, and this book contains the stories that were either written by themselves or others. Some say these stories are not true. Others believe them to be true accounts of what has happened over the years. If you would have read it before our recent trials and tribulations, you would have not taken the book seriously. You see now that more is possible than many humans realise, and so you may come to

1

believe in these stories, in the same way I do. Would you like to begin reading?"

Myasako said yes, and his father handed him a cloth to continue cleaning the book of its dust.

"I will tidy up in here," Kuyasaki said, looking at the mess around him. Myasako could see a trap door in the floor.

"I never knew that was there," Myasako said. "Did you?"

"Yes," Kuyasaki said, "but I never knew this book lay hidden within the walls beneath, until my master Hirozama came to me in a dream. He knew this place better than anyone."

"We will begin reading soon," Kuyasaki said. "Give me a few moments."

As Myasako went and sat at the table of another room, he opened up the book. There were twelve stories, all written by different people, and what he read with his father that day and in the weeks to come, will now be read by you...

Secrecy

*These are the ninja chronicles,
and to those of you who read,
be sure that you are not in sight
of any enemies.*

*If enemies can read this,
then they may sense our secrets,
and ninjas work and do work best
in darkness and concealment.*

*Keep this book well tucked away,
where no one thinks to look.
Our enemies will never know
the wonders of this book...*

3

These stories are arranged in the order that they were first recorded on paper.

The true sequence of the events is unknown.

Chapter 2 - The Lightning Ninja

The Lightning Ninja is one of the most ancient ninjas we know of. He was first discovered living in a small crater in the ground, surrounded by nothing but stones and leaves.

The first one to discover him was a boy named Terana.

Terana was walking beside a woodland on the edge of his village. He was alone. There had been a loud rainstorm in the night, branches had fallen from the trees, and as Terana walked along the edge of the woodland, he saw a small crater in the ground ahead of him.

He peered over the edge of the crater and looked down. A man was sitting there, meditating, dressed completely in grey and wearing a grey mask so that only his closed eyes could be seen. The crater was not wide, but it was deep.

"Hello?" Terana said. Terana lived in a very safe village, full of love, laughter and light. None of the villagers had ever experienced any violence, and so they were never warned to be wary of strangers.

"Hello?" Terana called down again at the ninja in the crater. Very slowly the man's masked face turned and looked up at Terana, and instantly Terana's mind was flooded with light, as if a bolt of lightning had just flashed through his brain. For a moment he could see nothing but bright white light, and when he could see clearly again, the ninja in the crater was gone.

When Terana returned home, he told his mother what happened over by the forest. She laughed.

"Disappeared, did he?" she said, smiling and serving him a plate of food from a pot she was holding. Terana lived in a small hut with his two parents. His father was outside chopping wood.

"Yes," Terana said, stunned that his own mother didn't believe what he was telling her. "He just vanished. The crater is still out there."

"I'm sure it is," Terana's mother said, as she finished serving his plate and began to walk away from the table. "I'm sure it is, Terana."

"I'm telling the truth!" Terana said. "Why don't you believe me?"

"I do," Terana's mother said, turning around and smiling at her son. "Of course I believe you."

*

That night Terana had a dream. He was angry that his mother wouldn't believe his story, and in his dream he took her out to the crater by the forest and showed her the man dressed in grey that was quietly sitting at the bottom of it.

"See!" Terana said to his mother. "Now do you see?"

"I don't see anything, Terana," his mother replied. "This is all just your imagination."

"He's there! He's right there!" Terana yelled, pointing, and just as he became so angry that he felt as if he was about to explode, Terana woke up, and it was raining again outside.

He heard thunder, there was a flash outside and Terana ran to his hole-in-the-wall which acted as a window. He removed the wooden board that was the cover, and he saw flash after flash of lightning striking the ground between the village and the trees of the forest, and every lightning strike made another crater in the ground. He knew he couldn't go outside, it was too dangerous, but he stood and watched for hours as he tried to see that mysterious man in grey walking around out there, or climbing out of holes in the ground.

The next morning, when the storm had passed, Terana ran out of his hut and sprinted towards the new group of craters in the ground. His mother followed after him, telling him to come back inside for breakfast.

He ignored her. Terana knew he would be punished for it, but he was consumed by the desire to find this man and prove his existence to his mother. He ran alongside the craters until he saw him again. In one of the holes in the ground, this man was sitting quietly, not doing anything at all.

"Who are you?" Terana said to him. "Who are you?"

The masked man slowly looked up at the boy from the bottom of the hole in the ground, and Terana was sure he could see this man's eyes begin to smile. The eyes were almost shining, and there was a strong kindness within them, mixed with an intense ferocity. Terana suddenly thought of a dragon, or a tiger – creatures he had been told about but had never encountered.

"I am the Lightning Ninja," the man said. Terana could hear his mother calling for him as she ran out of the village to chase him. "I keep your village, and other villages safe from harm."

"From lightning strikes?" Terana said.

"Yes, and other things."

"What other things?"

The Lightning Ninja turned his head to stare at the wall of earth in front of his face.

"There are things in those woods that are not the friendliest of creatures," he continued. "Some are human, some are not. I protect those villages that have managed to retain their innocence. I keep the peace, but I am not always peaceful."

"Terana!" his mother yelled as she approached him and grabbed him by the ear. She was holding a wooden spoon in her other hand. Terana's mind flashed with light again, and he pointed her attention down into the crater below them.

"Look," Terana said. "There he is."

"These are lightning bolt craters," she said. She had seen hundreds of them before. "So what?"

Terana stopped wincing for a moment as his mother still held on tight to his ear, and he looked down into the crater where he was pointing. The Lightning Ninja was gone, and all he could see was twigs and leaves.

"He was there," Terana said. "He was just there! The Lightning Ninja. He keeps us safe!"

"Safe from what?" his mother yelled, beginning to drag him back towards the village by his ear. "There's nothing to fear. The lightning never strikes us, and we are always very safe."

"But there's a reason!" Terana yelled, as his voice started to fade away from the ears of the forest. "There's a reason we live like this!"

"Come back inside, and don't ever disobey me when I call you home!"

Terana's mother dragged him back towards their hut, and Terana never saw the Lightning Ninja ever again.

Belief

Be mindful of your beliefs – if they are your own, or a product of what you have been taught by others.

The Lightning Ninja

There are very few tales of the Lightning Ninja ever being seen. It is thought that he dedicated his life to anonymously protecting those who he believed deserved it. People who have seen him believe he finds great joy in keeping people safe, and seeks in no way to be rewarded for his services.

Chapter 3 - The Legend Of Ninja Power

This is a legend, a warning,
to all ninjas who read.
If you are ever captured,
be sure you do not bleed.

If your blood is tasted
by your adversaries,
then they will take your power,
and weaken your bodies.

Once your blood is harvested,
your strength will not return.
Your blood may slowly rebuild but
your system will have learned...

It will sense that you are in
the hands of enemies,
your power is being stolen and
is in the hands of thieves...

So it will cease from blessing you
with power you can't keep,

instead of giving strength to thieves,
it will keep you weak.

In such a situation,
you must then depend
on ninjas you have taught
to empower and defend.

If you have helped to forge
fellow ninjas with great skill,
then they will come to help you,
when nobody else will...

Chapter 4 - Three Young Ninjas

"No Ninjas Allowed" was the sign written at the entrance to the town. The three ninjas stood there, in normal clothes, and they did not even stop to read it. They all saw the sign, but they kept on walking as if the words meant nothing to them.

They walked through the town. It was an ancient, rural town with dusty roads and old timbered buildings, with elderly ladies sitting outside their homes on rocking chairs, and women tending to their children and babies who were either crying or running around outside. There was a tavern in the distance, and the three ninjas were hungry.

"I hope they have fish," one of the ninjas said. His name was Fanza. Fanza was a large, round, heavy young man who could never lose weight, no matter how hard he tried. He trained with the other two, ate healthily like the other two, but for some reason could not shift the fat away from his flesh. He looked as if he was a slow, lazy, good-for-nothing individual with no willpower or skills to speak of. But he was quite the opposite.

"Chicken. All I want is chicken." Another ninja said. His name was Stiko. Stiko was the same height as Fanza, a similarly young age, but he was skinny. He looked as if he would break if someone was to push him with enough force, and no matter how hard he tried, he could never put on weight. His arms and legs were long and sinewy, and to look at him you would think he was a weak, untrained, unskilled man with no strength or power to speak of. But he was quite the opposite.

"I just hope they have food," the final ninja said. This ninja was named Doroko. He was a strongly built machine of a young man who had to wear baggy clothes to try to conceal his muscles. He looked as if he came from a long line of great warriors who had been bred to conquer all adversaries in battle. He did not come from this kind of lineage, since ninjas were not bred for the battlefield, but there was a story about him that he always claimed no knowledge of. The story said that when he was a baby he was blessed by an ancient ninja, and that ninja proclaimed he would be the most ferocious ninja who ever lived.

The three ninjas walked past houses, and they could feel eyes looking at them.

"Outsiders!" one of the elderly women shouted. "Outsiders!"

A group of men came running out of a town hall. They were armed with rifles.

"Outsiders?" one of them shouted. "Who goes there?"

The three ninjas put their hands up.

"We are just three men, looking for food," Fanza said.

"It looks like you've had plenty already," the leader of the men said. He pointed his rifle at Fanza's belly, and all the men behind him laughed.

"Please," Doroko said. "We have just come for something to eat. We have money to pay. That's all we have come for. Perhaps we will rent a room for a night, and then we will be on our way. We are just passing through."

The leader of the men in the town had a large moustache, and he was wearing a fine suit. He pointed his rifle up at the sky, and he inspected the three ninjas.

"You know..." the moustached man said, taking a few steps towards the ninjas, as the other townsmen still had their rifles at the ready. "We've had some trouble over recent months. Ninjas. Ninjas have been coming here, stealing our food and drink and then running off into the night. Thieves, the ninjas are, nothing but thieves."

Stiko, the skinny ninja, grabbed Fanza by the forearms as he sensed Fanza beginning to lose all control of his emotions. Fanza's father had once been captured in this town, and after years of imprisonment had managed to escape.

"Yes, yes, we have heard about them too," Doroko said. "We will be the first to help out if any are spotted while we are here."

The man with the moustache stared for a while, and his moustache twitched.

"It's very hard to tell a ninja, you know," he said, beginning to walk around the three ninjas. "They are taught to disguise themselves, to blend in wherever they go. We might as well just call them *thieves*, instead of ninjas. They lost their honour a long time ago."

Stiko grabbed Fanza even tighter and put Fanza's arm behind his back to restrain him.

"Okay," the man said, waving at his team of men to lower their weapons. "On your way. But we keep track of all outsiders. You will be watched while you are here."

"Very well," Doroko said, putting his hands together in thanks. His body was about twice the width of Stiko. "We'll be on our way then, thank you."

The three ninjas began to walk, through the crowd of rifled men, and they made their way towards the tavern ahead of them.

*

That night the three ninjas were staying at an inn. They had paid for three rooms, and had met in Doroko's room late at night.

"Where is it, then?" Fanza whispered. "I couldn't see a sign of it anywhere."

"I think it's underground," Stiko said. "Something tells me there must be a tunnel somewhere."

"We have to be patient," Doroko said. The bed looked as if it was being crushed beneath him as he sat on it. "We have to wait for it to appear to us."

"We cannot wait!" Stiko said. "He might be suffering down there, if our fathers' stories are anything to go by. "

"He might not even be down there now. We don't know, do we?" Doroko said.

Stiko was irritated. He felt so close, and yet so far away from saving someone he cared so much about. As Stiko stared at Doroko with piercing eyes, Doroko realised there was no time to waste.

"Let's go, tonight," Doroko said. "Where is the man who was standing outside of your room, Fanza?"

"He's tied up in the bath," Fanza said.

"And yours, Stiko?"

"In the bath too. I put some sleeping salts in there with him."

"Well, okay then," Doroko said. "Let's wake up this one, and we'll ask him some questions."

Doroko started to shake the man who was tied up on the floor of his room, the one that had been standing outside his door all night to see if Doroko ever left, and Doroko had some questions he wanted to ask...

*

After the questioning, which was eventually successful, the three ninjas made their way down to the basement of the hotel. The corridors were empty and the stairs were quiet, all until they reached the laundry room.

There were workers down there, washing sheets and squeezing them dry over and over again. There was another staircase going down outside the entrance to the laundry room, and Doroko began to creep down the stairs, carefully.

There was no sound, and the workers in the laundry room heard nothing. Stiko followed and so did Fanza, and Fanza was so light on his feet that Stiko didn't even hear him breathe as he moved.

The ninjas kept running down the dark stairs, so silently that it was as if they were at one with the steps beneath them. When they reached the bottom of the stairs, Doroko peered around the corner to see a short corridor with a door at the end, with two armed guards standing either side of the door. It was dark, with a few flaming torches on the walls, and the guards had not noticed or heard the ninjas in the shadows.

The ninjas said nothing, but Doroko pointed towards the door and made a strange sign with two of his fingers to indicate two guards were standing there.

Stiko took out a little metal ball from his pocket, slowly looked around the corner at the guards in the distance, and then threw the ball so that it landed on the door behind them. It made a sharp clinking noise, the guards turned to pursue the sound, and soon they were struck from behind, disarmed, and Stiko's sleeping salts were placed inside their noses. Now the ninjas were closer to their target, and the three of them disappeared into darkness as they took a key from a guard's waist, and opened the door leading even further underground.

They were not able to speak, but they could hear groans coming from down beneath them.

As the three ninjas tiptoed along an iron bridge in darkness, they looked down below and could see three cages illumined by candlelight, and in the middle there was a man clinging to the bars.

"No more. No more, please," the man said. He was skinny and gaunt with long hair and a beard, and standing in front of him were two men dressed in black.

"There's more in you, yet," one of the men said. "This ninja blood replenishes itself faster than any other."

The man dressed in black picked up a needle with a long thin tube coming out of the other end, and he made his way towards the man in the middle cage. "No, no," the caged man said. "No I can't lose any more blood. No, please, no."

As the man dressed in black with the needle opened the cage door, his friend behind him yelped and hit the ground. The man with the needle spun around, and felt the bottom of Fanza's foot driving straight into the centre of his face, breaking his nose and rattling his brain into the walls of his skull.

The man's head snapped back and he fell to the floor, hitting his head, and the three ninjas entered the cage to see their master.

"Master Shengzen," Doroko said.

"I knew you would one day come," their master said. "Thank you, thank you boys."

Doroko lifted up his master to lie over his shoulders.

"Are the other cages empty?" Stiko said. The cages on both sides of them looked darker than the middle one. There were patches where no light wanted to rest.

"No, they are not empty. They have two young girls in there. They are not ninjas like us. They are something else, something I have never seen, but they cannot move into the light. They can only dwell in darkness, or else they perish."

"Are they safe?" Fanza said, starting to become more jumpy.

"I have spoken to them before," their master said. "They seek vengeance against those who captured them."

"Let's release them," Stiko said.

"The keys," their master said. "The keys are with one of the other men."

Fanza ran to get the keys from the man dressed in black he had just knocked out.

"Take a lamp with us," their master muttered, seeming to become weaker. "If we carry a lamp then the girls will not harm us by accident."

Stiko picked up a flaming lamp from the wall and brought it over to Fanza who was preparing to unlock the first cage. Doroko blew out the other lamps on the walls so that there was complete darkness everywhere else.

As Fanza opened the first cage door and then the second, they all heard scurrying, a screeching, and a 'thank you' and these little girls ran past them and up the steps towards the entrance to the dungeon, and as the ninjas ran up the steps and followed, they began to hear screams of men in the town, as the girls were let loose on their capturers.

Loyalty

Loyalty is won by those who are worthy of trust.

Master Shengzen

Master Shengzen was famous for sacrificing himself for three other ninjas. On sensing their capture years ago, he wandered the land for months searching for them. He discovered his three students in cages, being kept alive for blood harvesting, and in freeing them all he was captured himself. When the three permanently weakened but liberated ninjas returned home, they told the story to their sons, who as soon as they were strong enough, left the safety of their own village and went to free their master for good. Stiko, Fanza and Doroko succeeded in their mission, and Master Shengzen lived happily for many years after.

Chapter 5 - The Forbidden Ninja

By Yinli Tenora

In my town it was forbidden for women to become ninjas. There were rumours of lands far away where they would recruit young female prodigies to become true ninjas, but we had no such luck where I was from. Where I lived everyone only wanted me to be safe.

I came from a rich family. I didn't appreciate it at the time. It was so normal that I assumed everyone just lived like that. My house was like a palace, I was waited on hand and foot by staff who would bring me anything I wanted at any time. My father was often busy with work, and my mother was often busy doing nothing, not very much interested in me, relaying my wants and needs to the staff that they had working around the clock in our home.

I wasn't let outside of the grounds until I was sixteen. Even then, security guards would assist me. I lived like royalty, but perhaps even more sheltered and protected, and it wasn't until I saw the harsher realities of my town, that I decided I wanted to be a ninja.

I wanted to go shopping in the town. It took me three days to have my request granted. I was told over and over again that they could go out and get anything I wanted for me, but I wanted to experience it for myself. I had never bought anything in a shop. I didn't know where clothes and jewellery and food even really came from. I was becoming curious, feeling as if I had been trapped in a golden prison where instead of inmates looking to harm me or steal my possessions, I was surrounded by loyal servants.

I should have been more appreciative. I certainly was after I was taken out into the town. As we walked through dirty streets – me and five large men who were my bodyguards – I looked through the gaps in between their bodies to see women in the market stooped over low and trying to peer in at me through those same gaps. Everyone looked dirty, their clothes looked old, there was a sense of hustle and struggle in the air that I was not used to at all. And then we heard them shouting.

A group of men ahead of us had seen us. They knew it was me, the daughter of the richest man in town. No other woman would be able to afford so many guards. It was no secret amongst these people that anyone who was able to get their hands on me would be able to charge any ransom they wanted for me to be returned safely to my prestigious home. And they went for me that day.

There was suddenly a huge brawl. Men attacked my security guards with machetes and knives. My security guards fought so efficiently that soon all of the attacking men were falling down with their own weapons stuck inside them. I watched as women screamed and children cried, and more and more men started to pile into the narrow market to try to grab me. Soon they became too much. Thirty, then forty men were in the village piling on top of the security guards who were now struggling to keep them off. One of my guards was pulled away from me, and I felt a thin, wiry and dirty hand grab at my wrist, and I didn't know what to do. In the panic of it all I put my teeth to his fingers and started to bite as hard as I could. I felt something warm start to burst out of the fingers, and the hand released me. Now it was chaos everywhere, bodies fighting and stabbing everywhere around me, and as I saw men's eyes start to turn towards me, I saw a little old lady sitting calmly by a wall close by, next to a dark, empty hole in the brickwork. She nodded at me, so serenely, and she beckoned me towards her with one hand. She was holding a cigarette in the other.

I didn't know what was on the other side of that dark hole, but men started to lunge at me through the gaps that were now forming in between all of my guards. The woman looked far more friendly than all of these men, so I ran, I ran for the hole in the wall, and as I squeezed through fighting bodies and kicked away at something trying to grab my ankle, I dove into that dark hole in the wall, and had no idea where I was going to land.

I quickly landed on hard ground, I didn't know how to roll or fall properly so I scraped my knees and wrists on the dirty floor. I looked behind me and could see out into the marketplace, men from the town were turning away from the melee and trying to chase me in to where I was now crouching. For some reason, they couldn't fit through the gap in the wall. Perhaps it was the perfect size for me, or perhaps it was a magic wall. In any case, I watched as men stuck their arms through the gap and tried to climb their way in. They couldn't. Other men would try, all at the same time, sticking legs and heads and hands and feet through the space, but no-one could get through. I stood and took a little step back, and stepped on something hard that clinked beneath my foot. I looked down and it was a sword. I picked it up. I felt tremendously powerful, all of a sudden. It was as if the sword had a mind of its own. It *wanted* to cut through the men that were trying to capture me. It *wanted* to slice and cut and tear at any limb of anyone that was trying to harm its new master. I took a step forward, then another one, and then another one until I was at the side of the hole in the wall, and arms were still reaching through the gap, scratching at the floor.

"She's just inside there!"

"She jumped through!"

"Why can we not fit?!"

I raised the sword above my head, but it felt as if it was raising itself. It was as if it was now attached to my nervous system, controlling every movement I was making.

And then just as I wanted to cut down at any limb that was trying to struggle through that gap, a hand caught my elbow and stopped me.

"Release the sword," someone said.

The hand squeezed my elbow and it took all the strength from my arms. I dropped the sword, it clattered to the ground, and that old lady from outside the wall bent over and picked it up.

"You are not ready for this yet," she said. "I didn't know it had made its way in here."

She stepped back into the darkness.

"How...how did you get in here?" I said. "I didn't see you."

"You shouldn't see me. Especially when I'm sneaking," she said. "The true ninjas are only seen when they want to be seen."

I looked at her. She was not smoking now. I could only see the outline of her old body, which was now standing up unusually straight. The sword slightly glinted at her side, and she was wearing old brown rags for clothes.

"You?" I said. "You're a ninja?"

She didn't respond.

"I've heard of them, I've read about them," I said. "I didn't know they were real. What do they actually do?"

"We are trained for spying, assassinating, collecting information, even stealing," she said. She still hadn't moved. "But the true ninja way is much deeper than the tasks we are trained to carry out. The *true* ninja way makes you a master of yourself, and subservient to no one else."

I took a step towards her.

"The ninja way has been twisted over the years," she said. "Now they say the true ninjas are the ones who serve a master, usually a master that is only interested in the welfare of a select few. The original spirit of the ninja way is to become an incorruptible force within yourself that lives a powerful and free life."

The noise from the fighting crowd outside seemed to no longer be important. I wanted to hear more.

"You mustn't stay here," the old lady said. "Your parents will be worried."

"No they won't," I said. "They don't really care about me. My father's always too busy, my mother doesn't spend much time with me."

"They will still be worried. You must return to them."

"I don't want to now," I said. "I want to be a ninja. Are you really a ninja?" I was having trouble getting my mind around the idea. She looked so old, so normal.

"Real ninjas don't stand out at all. That's the whole point of them," she said. She disappeared and then spoke from behind me.

"Ninjas are completely stealthy, bred to blend with everything around them."

I spun around and saw her there, still with the sword, smiling.

"I want to train with you, I want to learn from you!" I said.

"I will handle the crowd outside," she replied. Her voice was deep and raspy. "Then you will climb back out into the market and return home to your parents. If you are serious about training with me, it will be a full-time commitment. I will speak to you when you are back at home."

"How?" I asked.

"You will see," she said.

She vanished again, and I heard the noise from outside suddenly begin to die down. The screaming stopped, the shouting stopped, the crying stopped. Hands and feet withdrew themselves from the gap in the wall, and everything became quiet.

"Yinli? Yinli?" I heard one of my guards calling me. I climbed out through the gap in the wall, and everything appeared very normal. It was as if there had never been any kind of fighting going on. Market sellers were selling, children were running, people were buying things...my guards looked smart and unscathed.

"How did you manage to sneak off?" my guard said. His name was Henshin, the strongest of my guards, who was always very stern with me.

"Never mind," I said. "Are you all okay? How did all the fighting stop?"

He paused. "What?" he said. "What fighting?"

"I want to go home now," I said. "I don't want to shop anymore. Please, let's go home."

"Very well." Henshin took me by the arm and led me back to the enclosed circle of guards around me, and as we walked off back to my horse and carriage, I saw the old lady by a market stand, just for a moment, and she winked at me.

*

I didn't tell my parents anything when I got home. I was too afraid they'd think I was crazy. I was starting to think I was too. Had I imagined all of that? The fight, the lady by the hole in the wall? I couldn't figure out what happened, but when my father got home, I told him something.

"Father, I want to be a ninja."

He snorted. He was back for the evening, standing at the kitchen counter drinking something.

"Never," he said. "You live too much of a privileged life. The only ninjas in existence have only come from poor families who needed extra ways to make money. We have plenty, so you don't have to do that."

"What if I wanted to? What if I *really* wanted to be a ninja, not to serve any leader or politician, but to develop myself fully from within?"

He looked at me. He hadn't looked at me so directly in years. At least I had his attention for a moment.

"What? We are doing everything so that you can do that already! You have the finest education, you have every possible resource at your disposal, the library is filled with..."

"But you know yourself that *doing* things is what helps you to grow the most," I said. I didn't know where all these words were coming from. "You didn't have the finest schooling, father, but you did well..."

"And I'm giving you what I didn't have so that you may do even better!" he snapped. "Now it's getting late. Go to bed. You will never be a ninja. Not ever. Not only will I not allow it, you are not strong enough to do such a demanding job."

I stormed off. I had never felt more sure that I was going to do it, if indeed I wasn't crazy. If I had imagined the whole thing back at the market, if it was all just some kind of strange hallucination, then at least I had experienced something different for a change. I went to bed that night, and spent most of my time staring at the darkness of my ceiling.

I managed to fall asleep eventually and I saw her again. The old woman was standing in front of me, at the foot of my bed. I didn't know I was dreaming at the time. It seemed too real.

"What did they say?" she asked me.

"I didn't tell anyone about what happened in the market. Am I going insane?" I said. "When I left you, it was like nothing ever happened out there."

"I told you I would take care of it," she said, smiling slightly.

"How, how did you manage to reverse everything, so that no one even remembered, or had any scratches or cuts or dirt on them from all the fighting?"

"I'm experienced," she said. "The mind is far more powerful than most people realise."

I stared at her face. It was still quite dark. I could see some wrinkles.

"So will they let you train as a ninja?" she said. I felt she already knew the answer.

"I didn't even ask my mother." I said. "My father said no. Absolutely not."

"How old are you?"

"Sixteen."

"Hmm," the woman said. "At what age are you allowed to leave school?"

"Sixteen. But my parents would never let me out of education."

"Hmmm," she said again. "I believe sixteen should be an independent age, if the individual is ready. You must sit your parents down and tell them what is going to happen. Either you come and train with me, full-time as a ninja, where you can carry on with your education. Or, you just carry on with your life as normal, as if we had never met. Which do you choose?"

"I choose the way of the ninja," I said, "but my parents, they won't let me. They won't let me out of the house again if I say that, and how could I possibly continue my education? Do you mean bring teachers with me to where you are? Where would I meet you? Would you come here?"

"Just tell them your choice. Just tell them that next week you will begin your training. Just tell them. It is not fair to keep them in the dark. At least tell them. Be honest and clear."

The woman vanished, and I woke up, still in the darkness of the night, still with so many questions filling my head.

*

I had written everything down, every question I had, and I had written out my objective for the next day underneath everything:

"Tell my parents what I want to do."

I didn't like the idea of it. They would make me feel terrible about it, they would have so many questions for me as well, they would make me feel as if I was bad for wanting to train as a true ninja. But I knew I had to do it.

I caught them both in the morning before my father left for work. My mother was staring into the kitchen counter. I think she might have been on some sort of drug.

"Mum, Dad, I need to tell you something," I said. I was shaking slightly. I knew I was going to sound crazy. "Next week I start ninja training. My education will carry on, but I will be training as a ninja."

My father huffed. He just wanted to go to work.

"And how will you do that?" he said, closing his briefcase and standing up to leave.

"I'm just telling you, I have to tell you. Next week I start my training."

"Okay," he said. "Well you can always use the gymnasium downstairs. I've never seen you use it much before. I don't know if leaving the house was very good for you. It's given you some strange ideas about what you want to do with your life. Anyway, I have to go."

"Mum, did you hear me?" I said. She turned and looked at me slowly.

"You should do whatever you want," she said. She had a pale face. She stood up, walked out of the room, and walked upstairs back to bed.

*

The next few days were very normal. It was the weekend, and I spent my time either in my room or playing in the garden with some of my security guards. All of my schooling was done at home, so I didn't know what it was like to have friends my age.

"I might be going away soon," I said to Henshin, my head guard who was playing catch with me.

"Where?" he said.

"To be a ninja," I said.

He laughed very slightly. "Okay," he said, playing along. "Where?"

"I don't know. I just don't want you to be worried. If I disappear next week, I will be somewhere else, training."

"What, you'll sneak out of here, will you?" Henshin smiled. "Under our watchful eye? You know that's not possible."

"I'm just telling you," I said. "I'm telling everyone. Don't worry about me if I suddenly disappear."

*

When Sunday evening came, I felt very excited. I didn't know what was going to happen, but I knew I was going to hear from the old lady again. My father had even spoke to me again that weekend, and explained to me the laws behind females becoming ninjas. In our town it was completely illegal, and he made sure I knew it was forbidden.

"There is no way you can actually be one," he had said to me. "I know you aren't completely serious about all of this, but I have to tell you so that you don't get your hopes up."

I could have explained to him that I wasn't interested in the *job* of being a ninja, but that I wanted to learn the *way* of the ninja. But I didn't. It was not worth the energy.

"I'm starting next week," was all I said, and he walked off in a slightly angry mood.

I stayed awake all of Sunday night, and didn't see her at all. When I fell asleep in the early hours of Monday morning, there was still no sign of the lady. I was starting to think again that I was indeed becoming a crazy young girl with imaginary friends.

Monday passed. I did my schoolwork with my two usual teachers. I was feeling a depression start to grip me. I thought I might have to be committed to some kind of psychiatric hospital to be checked out. Perhaps it really was all in my head.

Then that evening, I heard the guards start to talk amongst themselves in the house.

"There's an old lady standing at the gates. She's been there for half an hour."

I ran to the kitchen window and saw her standing there. It was her. She wasn't moving, but as I appeared at the front door of the house she started to wave.

"Yinli, get away from there!" one of the guards shouted at me.

I wanted to run out of the house and run towards her, but my guard picked me up and took me upstairs to my room.

"She's here for me!" I cried out. "She's come to collect me for ninja training!"

My guard put me down in my bedroom, walked out and closed the door behind him.

"Stay away from your window!" he ordered me before he left, and I sat in the middle of my room, doing nothing.

After a few seconds, when the guard had not opened my door again to check I was being obedient, I looked towards my window. I didn't feel in danger. I stood to my feet and walked over to it.

I looked out the window and saw two guards standing there, talking to the old lady. I opened the window to try to listen, and I could hear a faint outline of what they were saying.

"Please let me in," the lady said.

"No. Why?" Henshin said to her.

"I've come for the girl, Yinli."

Suddenly the guards both flinched, and they took out weapons.

"Get on the ground!" they both said. "No one threatens the girl!"

The old lady put her hands up.

"I am taking her to where she needs to be. She has chosen her path already. She will be safe with me."

And then the lady disappeared.

"Hello," she said, standing behind me. I jumped and clutched at my chest.

"Are you sure you want to do this?" she said to me. "How can you trust me?" I could see her better in the light of my bedroom. She had neat grey hair tied back behind her head, and a fierceness in her eyes that looked as if it could accomplish anything.

"You saved me from getting snatched away by those men in the town," I said. "If you wanted to harm me, you could have done it with that sword already, when we were behind the wall."

"If you take my hand, your training will begin," she said. "The choice is yours."

She held out her hand. It was wrinkled and leathery. I took a breath, held her hand, and I disappeared into nothing.

*

It was nice to be nothing. I felt totally free, boundless, endless and without limit. I don't know how long I was nothing for, but in front of my eyes the world seemed to take shape again. I was standing at the top of a mountain, overlooking a huge valley with the town in the distance.

The old lady was standing next to me, smiling slightly.

"The first thing you must conquer is your fear of death," she said.

"Okay," I said. "How?" I could feel a light breeze blowing against my skin, and suddenly I felt very short of breath.

"You have to jump. Jump off the edge of this mountain. Over there," she pointed.

She was pointing to a ledge for me to jump off. I absolutely refused.

"No way," I said, "that would actually be killing myself, wouldn't it? I'm not doing it."

"Very good," the old lady said. "You are not too obedient yet. You didn't even hesitate. That is an excellent place for us to start. The first lesson is: *never follow advice if it doesn't ring true in your heart.*"

I looked out over the view.

"Everyone has opinions," she said. "Lots of people think they know things when they don't. There are some who give very good advice, and you will probably be able to tell which ones they are. Their words will make sense, or you will know deep down that what they are saying is true."

"How can you ever really know who is right and who is wrong?" I said, thinking about my own parents.

"You never really can. You just have to use your own intuition."

Intuition was something I had never learnt about. I barely knew what it was.

"It's a bit like your gut feeling," she said. "We will develop your intuition into something that is known as 'the ninja sense', where you can sense what is about to happen, or what the best course of action is. Thinking is not really involved, it is more of a knowing."

"Okay," I said. "How long will all of our training last?"

She was silent for a moment.

"I have no idea," she said.

"Doesn't your intuition tell you anything?" I asked.

"Not yet," she said. "I don't think it really matters, do you?"

"Yes, I do," I said. "Of course it does. I don't want to be training my whole life. What would I be training for if my training lasted forever?"

"Ah," she said. "And so we step into the second lesson..."

*

Ninja training was not what I thought it would be. It was almost like being back with my school teachers, except instead of being at a desk indoors, I was now sitting on top of a mountain. The old lady had been telling me that training in the ninja way was a lifelong commitment.

"Training must be done for the love of itself, not just for some future gain," she said. *"Training will not last unless it is enjoyed."*

"Let's start then!" I said. "Let's actually do something. I want to learn how to develop these amazing powers like you have."

"That might take a lifetime," the old lady said. "It took me sixty years to do what I can do now."

I felt disheartened. Perhaps I should have just stayed at home.

"There is a realm within this mountain that is designed to develop your ninja skills," she said. But it isn't for the faint of heart. You can train with me for a while to build your strength before you enter the training realm, or you can dive right in. What do you want to do?"

I felt itchy. I didn't want to wait for anything. I had not learnt patience. But I also became fearful, all of a sudden.

"Train with you," I said.

"Okay, that is a wise choice," she said. "Scared, aren't you?"

"No," I said.

"You are, you're scared."

"I'm not," I said. I was lying. I wanted to go back home now.

"If you weren't scared then you would be eager," the old woman said. "Suddenly you look frozen."

"Alright I'm scared!" I snapped. "I don't know what this 'realm' you're talking about even is. Of course I'm afraid."

"Very good," she said. "Lesson number three – *fear is your friend*. Fear keeps you safe. Develop a friendly relationship with fear, rather than being embarrassed about it. Then it will not strangle you in your life."

I breathed a sigh of relief.

"Now the training begins," she said.

*

I trained with this lady for weeks. She wouldn't tell me her name. She could run so fast and for so long that I was always struggling to keep up. She could sprint up that mountain as if she wasn't even human, and when she began showing me some grappling techniques, she could pick me up with ease.

"Learn how to fall correctly, first," she said to me.

I spent days and then weeks learning how to fall before I learnt how to do anything else. After dedicating so much time to learning how to fall correctly, I felt almost indestructible.

"Now fighting techniques," she said. We spent more weeks together while she taught me how to kick, punch, and fight as well as she could. I still had a lot to learn, but by the end of the month, I felt as if I was a new woman.

"You have made great progress," she said. "Your family are still looking for you, but they are saving the letters you have been sending them, reassuring them of your wellbeing."

"How long before they look for us out here?"

"Two weeks," the lady said. "They will be here in two weeks. I think you are ready for your first trial. Follow me."

She led me down the mountain and through caves that she had never shown me before. For some reason I never needed much to eat when we stayed in this mountain. There was something so nourishing about its energy that all I needed was to drink from its spring a few times a day, and to eat the wild plants that grew near the base of the mountain.

"I know we haven't been following a traditional education plan recently," the old lady said. "But learning to live with nature is probably the most valuable education you can attain."

"Here," she said, pointing into a dark tunnel that was gently glowing with red within one of the caves. "Crawl through this tunnel, and you will enter your first trial."

"How dangerous is it?" I asked.

"It depends on your mindset. This trial will reflect your own mind back to you, your own deepest fears and negative energies will be thrown at you from all angles, as if these things exist outside of you. It is a test of mental strength more than anything else. You will have to learn as you go. Remember – what you resist within yourself will persist. Non-resistance is the key to transmutation."

"Okay," I said. I got on my hands and knees, and I felt a red warmth pulling me towards the dark and glowing tunnel, and I left the old lady behind.

The crawl through the tunnel did not last long. After a few seconds I felt my body gently disintegrating, as if every atom of every cell of my body was surrendering to a force much greater than itself, and suddenly I was formless again, without limit, and I felt a blissful feeling run throughout everything that I thought of as 'me'.

That didn't last long either. Suddenly I was standing in a forest, a dark forest, looking around at trees that seemed to be staring at me, telling me that this was no place for a teenage girl to be by herself.

Something grabbed me around the neck. I dropped my weight, loosened its grip with my hands and threw it over my back. It was a man, a man that looked very similar to one I had seen try to snatch at me in the market, and as he landed on his back he wheezed, and he began struggling for breath.

"That was too hard," he said. "Too hard."

"Don't touch me again," I said, and I wondered if I would ever escape this place.

"Yinli? Yinli?" I heard my mother calling. I followed the direction of her voice, but I couldn't see her. I could just see dark trees, warning me that I shouldn't be in a place like this. The ground beneath my feet felt dense with fallen twigs and old leaves.

Then I saw her.

"Yinli! Yinli over here!"

I could see my mother, stuck inside the ground. Only the top half of her body was visible. I ran over to her and she was stuck inside a thick sludge. It looked like quicksand, but it was more of a muddy swamp that she was trapped in.

"Get me out," she said. "You need to get me out."

"How?" I said. I started looking around for branches to pull her in with.

"I should have never married your father," she said. "I'm bored, unappreciated. I have no life."

I stared at her.

"That's not Father's fault," I said. "He doesn't stop you from doing things, does he?"

"I need support. I supported him for so long. He isn't interested in me."

I stared at her again. I didn't know what to say.

"Maybe you need to stop giving all of your power away to him," I suddenly said. Words seemed to be flowing out of my chest and through my mouth. "If you think you need everything from him before you can be happy, then you'll be waiting for him forever. You are strong, Mother, I know you are. I remember a time when you were happy and strong. Take your power back. Be self-reliant again."

She stared back at me, she nodded, and then she was sucked down into the earth completely, disappearing from my sight.

"Mother!" I said. I was so confused. It shouldn't have seemed so real, but it did. I was questioning whether it was. I was *sure* that it was my mother, a deeper version of her that I rarely got to see.

"She'll be fine," someone said. I turned around and saw my father standing there, reading a newspaper.

"Have you always ignored her like you do now?" I said to him.

"What are you talking about?" he said, ruffling the papers slightly as he continued to read. He always furrowed his brow when he read, and there was a permanent line between his eyebrows from the constant strain. His skin was dark and tough.

"You barely pay her any attention," I said. "You ignore her."

"I don't. I don't...do I?"

"Yes," I said. "Completely."

"Well...well..."

"Don't try to make excuses," I said. "Just be aware of it. Notice how much you've been ignoring her recently. Then things will change."

He ruffled his papers again, and as I blinked, he vanished.

Something else grabbed me from behind. I did the same thing, I broke its grip and threw it onto the ground.

Now I saw myself, lying there, unconscious.

I heard a rumbling sound. I could feel it in my feet. I looked around and there were thousands of me, all charging in and starting to scream things at me.

"You aren't good enough!"

"No one really likes you!"

"Your life isn't worth anything!"

"Your future will be empty!"

They were all charging at me and I started to run away.

"Your parents don't love you!"

"You are all alone!"

Every version of me was shouting something different. It was every bad thought I'd ever had about myself.

"Your parents don't get on well because of *you*. It's *your* fault! They were fine before *you* came along!"

I hated it. I hated the voices. I kept running and running and running, until I couldn't run for much longer. My legs and chest and heart and arms were burning, I was struggling to breathe, I felt my legs slowing down, even though I wanted to get away.

"You should have never been born!"

I turned and faced them all, exhausted from all the running, and as I surrendered and realised that I could not keep running, I opened my arms and welcomed all of them, every version of myself that I didn't like, or every part of myself that didn't like me. I welcomed all of them, I let them all in, and then a funny thing happened.

"What are you doing?" one of them said. "Why aren't you running?"

"I can't anymore. I'm tired of running," I said. "Come here, give me a hug."

The one version of myself I was talking to screwed up her face, disgusted, and then she vanished.

"Come on," I said to all of them. "Come here. Come to me."

"No," they all said. They all started to back away.

I had energy again.

"Come to me," I said. "I'm not scared of you anymore. You are all just thoughts, thoughts that need to be loved."

"No!" they all started to shout. As they backed away they began to turn and run.

"Come, come to me!" I called after them, and as I ran after them to chase them down, thousands of me were running away, and as they ran, they started to disappear.

They started to pop and vanish and fizzle away, and soon I was just running again, alone, but free, and the forest looked like a much friendlier place. The trees seemed golden and the air smelt fresh and the birds were singing loudly over my head.

"You're doing very well," I heard the old lady say. "Your training is now well underway."

Reward

Those who follow their true path will be rewarded.

The Forbidden Ninja

The ninja way accepts all people. All that is required is a willingness to adapt to and accept the ninja way. Although forbidden in her culture, this young ninja found that the path becomes clear to all those who desire to walk it. The adventures of the Forbidden Ninja will continue in "The Ninja Chronicles Part 2", where she meets more young ninjas like herself, and they are asked to complete their very first mission against a monster in the forest...

Chapter 6 - Hirozama's Memories

by Hirozama Tenjin

I never wanted to be a ninja. I was forced into it. Born into it. I didn't want to spy or kill or steal information from anyone else. I wanted to be a farmer. But we had enough farmers, apparently.

I was called up from a very early age. My father would watch me sneaking up on birds on our farmland when I was a boy. I could sneak so quietly and smoothly that I could catch a bird in my bare hands. I quickly released them again without harming them. I just wanted to see if I could catch them.

"Hirozama! Come in here at once!" my father called. I was just about to catch another bird, a very small one, but as my father bellowed out of our house, the bird flew off.

"Coming," I said, disappointed.

I walked up towards my house and felt a strong sense of foreboding in my chest. Something was telling me that I shouldn't enter my own home. Something was in there, waiting for me. I stood there as if I was frozen. I didn't want to go in.

"Hirozama! Come in!" my father yelled.

He would try to beat me if I ever disobeyed him. Still, I didn't move.

"Hirozama!" my father came bursting out of the back door of our house and ran up towards me. He went to grab me and I evaded. He swung at thin air. I was behind him. He turned, and I was gone again, now at his side. I noticed that three men in dark suits were watching from the kitchen window as they saw my father running round in circles, swiping at the air and not able to come close to touching me. They started writing something down. My father stopped.

"I have a great opportunity for you!" he said. "These men want to give you a trial run in the special forces!"

He was out of breath, panting, looking at me as if he had done me a favour.

"I want to stay here," I said. "I want to stay here and farm with you. That's all I want."

"A farmer's life is a mediocre one!" my father snapped. "We are all farmers. Anyone can be a farmer. Not everyone can serve our country like you could. I told them about your ability to catch birds, I suggested you could be a ninja..."

"No!" I said. "No I don't want to work for them! They'll have me do bad things, dangerous things for myself and others. I can feel it. No. I refuse."

My father went to grab me and I moved again, and I began to run away, across our fields.

I made it to the woods. I didn't know what to do. I hadn't seen the men in suits start to chase me, but I felt as if I couldn't go back home. My own father had betrayed me. I had heard him talking to my mother at night about what a family could earn if a child of theirs was ever donated to serve the country. Especially if it was a ninja.

"True ninjas are rare," my father said to her one night. "If any child is ever accepted into their true ninja program, the family is then set for life. No more farming, no more need to work..."

"Don't talk like that!" my mother said. "Don't you talk like that in this house! Not another word."

"But if I just made one phone call!"

"Never!" my mother hissed, and she walked into another room and slammed the door.

I should have guessed then that my father was talking about me. I was too young to consider the possibility that he would have me sent away. I thought he was talking about other children, never his own. And now I was all alone.

I climbed a tree and sat there for a while. My mother had been out in the fields that day, and I had not seen her since the early morning. I tried to spot her through the trees that overlooked our farmland, but I couldn't see her anywhere.

And then I saw them coming. Not men in suits, but soldiers dressed in dark clothes and masks who were silently running across our fields. I could see my father and the three men in suits slowly walking behind them.

Then I heard my mother start to shout.

"No! Fenzchen! You promised me! You promised me you would not call them!"

I saw her come running from the right-hand side, in the fields, and as she went to stand in front of the running masked soldiers, they pushed her to the side.

I felt a fury bite at my chest. No one was to ever touch my mother like that. She went and grabbed a soldier by the arm, and he turned and pushed her to the ground.

I was eight years old at the time. So young that I knew nothing but a primal rage that rose up in me as I saw a man push my mother to the ground. I decided that I would kill him. All of a sudden my mission in life, my very purpose on this earth was to destroy the man that pushed over my mother.

I jumped down the tree and hit the ground. I had no clarity or calmness. I just attacked. I burst out of the trees as the men were approaching the woods, and I found myself able to do incredible things. My strength had never been enormous, but my speed and cunning were unusually high. As the first soldier went to grab me, I rolled. As another went to trip me with his legs, I jumped over them and rolled again, and soon I reached the feet of the man who had pushed my mother.

I drove my fist directly upwards into his groin, and his legs buckled. I jumped on his back and I started to strangle him.

The pressure I could exert on this man's neck was tremendous. Something was giving me such a squeezing power it felt as if I was an anaconda wrapped around its prey. I thought my strength was meagre, but suddenly it was huge. I could feel my arm start to slice into the man's throat, and he was clawing at my arm to try to pull it off.

Soon they all were. All the soldiers were grabbing me, trying to pull me away from my prey. I could feel the life leaving him.

"You will never touch my mother like that again," I whispered in his ear, so that only he could hear, and just as I heard one of the men in suits shout out, "Tranquilise him!" I felt the man's body go limp, and then something sharp flew into the back of my neck, and the world began to turn very dark.

*

When I woke up, I was on a bed. There was a bright light directly above me, and I didn't want to look at it.

I looked to my feet. They were strapped to the bed. So were my wrists. The room was white, and my father was sitting in a chair by the wall. He wasn't saying anything. He looked guilty.

"What am I doing here?" I said. I felt weak. I could barely speak.

My father was chewing on one of his fingers. He always did that when he was worried.

"I'm sorry, Hirozama," he said. "I thought it would be easier than that, you shouldn't have run away. I just want the best for you. You can grow up to be a hero for our country."

"You want the best for *you*," I said. "That's all you want."

The three men in suits walked in again. My father stood up. They walked in unison, almost as if they were part of the same organism, and the one in middle held a clipboard with writing on it.

They stopped by the side of my bed, and the one with the clipboard spoke.

"Hirozama Tenjin. You are hereby instated into the true ninja training program. Your fight with our soldiers was magnificent. You show tremendous promise, and you will be an asset to our cause."

"What cause?" I said.

They turned to my father. The man on the left took out a check book from his pocket and began to scribble on it.

"Here is the agreed fee, in full," the man said, handing it to my father.

My father took the check, looked at the money, and realised it didn't take away the guilt that was starting to eat away at his heart.

*

My father left that evening. He told me he would see me soon, that my mother would be waiting at home. I was gradually beginning to regain my strength, and I was still tied down to the bed.

"Release me," I said to one of the men in suits who had been standing by my bedside, staring at me.

"Release me," I said again.

The man in the suit sniffed and slightly laughed.

"You belong to us now," the man said. "There is no escape. You might as well surrender to it. Your training will begin tomorrow. If you resist, you will be drugged until you become compliant. You will learn to enjoy your time here with us."

"What do you want me for?" I asked.

"You will see," said the man. "You will see."

*

I had tried to struggle out of my restraints all night, but with no success. They had men standing by my bedside at all times, working shifts, big men with those same masks as the soldiers who came to capture me. If I would struggle too much, they would threaten to inject me with something.

"It will send you to sleep," they would say, as they tapped the syringe full of fluid to release any air bubbles.

"No, I will just sleep by myself," I would reply, and then I would pretend to drift into unconsciousness, all the time forming a plan in my mind, not only of how I would escape, but how I would get my revenge.

*

The next morning they had me training. They had me running, with my hands still tied behind my back.

"It's a safety precaution!" one of the men in suits said. The three of them were still standing together.

"I can't run properly," I replied.

"You will get used to it," he said.

They had me running around their compound with other masked soldiers. All of them were men. They told me they were testing my fitness. I was used to running around for fun, for hours, and as the masked soldiers began to collapse from exhaustion, I stood there, ready for more.

"Very good," one of the suited men said. It was the one that always stood in the middle. He had a plain and pale face, hollow eyes, and a small scar above the left side of his top lip.

"How do you feel?" he asked me.

"Ready to serve you," I said. I was learning already. Inside I felt as if I wanted to kill every man in that compound. On the outside, I wanted to avoid all injections, and make them feel as if they had me.

"Good," the man smiled. "You are seeing sense. Although all a bit too soon. What about your mother? Your father?"

"They have forgotten me," I said, "so I am forgetting about them. They sold me, so why should I want to be back with them? At least you will care for me here. This could be a good life, if I accept it."

The middle man smiled. He didn't have all of his teeth, but the ones he did have were jagged and yellow.

"Good," he said. "Very good."

*

Over time they began to trust me. After a month they released my handcuffs and even let me sleep with my hands free. A month after that I was allowed to sleep without restraints, but still with a masked guard always by my side, armed with a sword and knife, with more standing by my door.

After six months, they brought in a new recruit. It was a girl.

"No! No!" I heard her screaming down the corridor. So far my hospital-like room had been private. Now I would be sharing.

They wheeled her in. She was tied down to the bed, kicking and screaming and wailing. Her parents walked in behind the masked guards who were pushing her, and the mother was in tears.

The three suited men walked in after her, and I sat up and watched.

"I'm not sure this is the right decision!" the girl's mother said. She was crying, being held by her husband. I noticed that she had holes in her shoes.

"We need the money," I saw the husband whisper into her ear.

"But look at her!" the mother shrieked back. She went to unstrap her daughter but the husband held her back.

"She is gifted," the husband said. "She will get used to it. She could be honoured as a hero one day."

And then I saw something that nearly made me lose my cool, completely ruining the illusion that I had worked so hard to build up over the past six months. As the mother became more hysterical, I saw one of the suited men nod towards her. One of the masked soldiers responded to the nod by walking beside her, trying to restrain her, and he sneakily injected something into the side of her leg.

Her leg buckled, and the soldier quickly hid the syringe in his back pocket.

"There's a pain in my leg," she said, starting to fall to the ground. The husband lowered her down, starting to look panicked.

"It's okay," he said, "everything will be okay."

She went drowsy, and for a while all that anyone could hear was the relentless screams of their daughter, until the suited man nodded again, this time in the direction of the girl.

*

Three months later, I was trialled as the girl's night-time guard. They wanted me to convince her to do as she was told. I would sit by her bedside, unarmed, with armed guards standing by the door.

She was heavily drugged. She was refusing to comply with anything they asked of her.

She had enough energy to mutter, very quietly, and she stared at me for a while.

"You look too young," she said.

"I am," I whispered back. I turned and looked at the armed guards. They were out of whispering range.

"How long have you been here?" she asked.

67

"Nine months," I said.

"They broke you," she muttered.

"I will break *them*," I said.

And then she fell asleep.

*

After exactly one year of training, I was now deemed ready to carry out my own mission. I had spent months and months knowing that to blast my way out of the place would have been too dangerous, and that actually, the training I had been receiving was extremely beneficial. The physical training, the tactical advice that I had accessed was hugely advantageous for me. Enjoyable, even. It was their mental training that I did not like, that I had to pretend I was falling victim to.

They would have me hypnotised every morning. I soon had visions of what they would be doing in hundreds of years – having recruits staring at shining screens and listening to speeches that would drone through their ear pieces. But in the time period I found myself in, no such advancements were made.

They would *try* to hypnotise me. They would lull me into a deep sense of relaxation that I had to fake, and they would have me repeat affirmations that I had to disbelieve every time I spoke them.

68

Things like, *"I always follow my master's orders. The master is the ruler of all. I owe the master my life. My life's work is to protect and enforce the master's wishes."*

I had never met the master, but he was presented to me in the twelve months of training as some kind of god, some kind of ultimate protector that I had to become the servant of. I hated every moment of the mental training, but I knew that as I slept beside armed guards and saw them all surrounding the iron fences, that I had little option but to bide my time and seize the right moment when it came. And now it was coming.

I was sitting on my bed. The girl was gone, taken for hypnosis, and the three suited men were standing at the foot of my bed. Two armed guards stood either side of me.

"Your first mission will be acquisition," the suited man in the middle said. "It is an order that has come directly from the master himself."

"I will serve the master," I said, robotically.

"Yes, you will. Your orders are to attain information from a compound not dissimilar to this one. You will have to sneak in, and then sneak out."

"I will serve the master," I said again. "but...I need to practice. I must practice here, in this building, to be able to move undetected. Then I will be confident in serving the master to the fullest."

The suited men turned away from me to converse with each other. They seemed to forget that part of my training had been to strengthen my sense of hearing. I could hear every little word they were saying. They trusted me now, and they were willing to let me try something by myself.

They all turned back to face me. The middle one spoke.

"You will not be allowed to leave this compound alone to sneak back in," the middle man said. "But you will be given thirty minutes to see if you can sneak out. We will surround the border and watch for your emergence. If you are successful, you will be deemed fit for the operation."

"For the master," I said.

"For the master," he said.

*

That night I had a fantastic dream. My escape attempt was set for tomorrow, where every guard would be notified to try to detect me moving through the compound. My dream was so fantastic that it was as if there was no such thing as sleep. I felt as if I had stepped into a different dimension.

The dream took me through every piece of training I had ever received in that place. Every piece of knowledge, every second of fight training, every ounce of strength gained from their training programme. I realised that I had grown in strength and speed and fighting ability, but I had been taken further away from my natural instincts by their incessant mental training to turn me into a subservient slave.

A bird appeared in my dream, a great bird that looked like a grand version of the ones I used to catch on the farm.

"You have to keep what is useful, and discard what is useless," the bird said. It looked like a brown eagle. "You must keep your physical strength, but plug your mind back into your intuition. This education system has known nothing of the *true* ninja way, despite what they say. You must keep the knowledge they have taught you that is of benefit, and disregard anything that blocks you from using your true intuition."

"What is intuition?" I asked.

"It is the knowing that you have always felt deep inside your body," the eagle replied. "Follow your instincts."

71

The bird flew off away from my dream, and I felt my attention rest inside my heart.

I woke up at five a.m., as usual. I sat up. I was told that I could begin my attempt at any time after five.

Guards no longer stood at my bedside, but they stood at the door, and one stood beside the girl in front of me.

I sat up, and the guard by her bed ignored me.

I walked up to him, smoothly. He couldn't hear me.

"Tell those other guards to report to head office," I said. I whispered it very gently, but I imagined I was speaking it into the guard's soul.

"Yes, sir," the guard nodded. He bowed and went to speak with the guards at the door. They all began to walk away down the corridor.

The girl had seen what happened. She was awake, unusually wide-eyed.

"How did you do that?" she asked.

"My training. And my instinct," I said.

"It was as if you hypnotised him yourself," she said. "Did they teach you that?"

"Only by the way they tried to hypnotise *me*," I said. "I plan to leave this place for good. Right now. If I wait to escape until my real mission, they will probably have a team watching me all the time. Plus, if I escape now, I can take you with me."

The girl looked unsure. "Go without me," she said. "I'm too weak. I'm so full of drugs that I can't..."

Suddenly I felt something rising up from the ground, as if a golden power was shooting itself through my veins and bones. I touched her on the arm and she shot upright.

"What was that?" she said. "It felt like electricity."

"I don't know," I said. "Something's happening to me, stuff they never taught me is...it's starting to do things through me. I had a dream last night. I think something has changed..."

"You're a true ninja," she said "*a real* one, not an artificial one. A real one!"

"Let's go," I said.

She seemed to move even more silently than I did. We ran through corridors, and it was almost as if I could see through walls. I could sense where guards were, and she could too, and we would run further through corridors, bide our time and continue waiting until our path became clear.

"I feel like we need to go underground," she said. "I don't know why."

"Me too," I said, and once we found a stairwell, we went down, down, and further down until we reached a very dark and dank area of the building that did not look as if it had seen a person for many years.

*

We had both been told to never go so deep under the ground.

"*A true ninja never goes into the depths of this compound.*" They made me repeat that every day. The darkness of the depths of the building were made out to be scary, dangerous and to be avoided at all costs.

For some reason, I felt we should enter the darkness.

As soon as we left the staircase and began to walk into the dark space, we heard something laughing.

"Finally," a voice said. "Finally the true ninjas have arrived."

The floor lit up and we could see an outline of a spirit of an old man, silently sitting beside a candle. The spirit was shimmering. I felt a flash of fear.

"Very good," the spirit said. "Very good! You know that they can never mask the true ninja way. No matter what they do, they can not get rid of the depths of this building or block its path for long."

This spirit of a man had his eyes closed. He was thin, wearing a cloth around his waist. His legs were crossed.

"They have tried to get rid of this realm, but they cannot. They have built a whole compound to try to mask it, but it still draws the rare few ninjas in."

The man was smiling, shimmering still, and when he opened his eyes, golden light flooded out onto me. Suddenly I felt the presence of love.

"The suppression attempt will be foiled by those who enter the *true* ninja way," he said. "You two are fine examples. The true ninja creates a rebellion of peace and independence. What they teach now is used to enforce slavery."

"The master," I said. "They would tell us about the master. Who is that?"

"The true master is within you," the spirit said. "The true master, your true guide, is within. The master *they* speak of is a political figure. So political that few ever get to see him."

"And who are *you*?" the girl said. I still didn't know her name.

"I am a ninja who stays here to teach. I taught when I was a physical being, and I teach from non-physical. I began to teach such a rebellion against the powers of this world, that when I passed, they tried to build over everything I had given to this realm. But it will not last."

"How do we escape from here?" I asked.

"Continue walking on your path. Straight ahead," the spirit said.

"Into the darkness?"

"Into the light."

I couldn't see a light anywhere around us. There was only a light coming from his eyes, and the candle beside him.

"The light is within," the ninja said.

I closed my eyes, turned in and saw a golden light within myself that was so strong that it scared me.

"Yield to the light," I heard the ninja master say, and in a few moments I relaxed, and felt this light begin to submerge my entire mind and being.

"And now, you have real power," the spirit said.

Instinct

Learn to trust your instincts.

<u>Hirozama Tenjin</u>

Hirozama Tenjin was an accidental ninja, but later grew to become legendary at a very early age. His powers gradually began to transcend the expected limitations of the physical realm, and the challenges he met later in life forced him to grow even stronger. The girl he meets in this story, named Enora Siygan, was known as the most gifted ninja in our history, possessing powers that other ninjas took years of practice to develop. Her adventures alongside Hirozama will continue in "The Ninja Chronicles Part 2".

Chapter 7 - Henrik The Defender

Before he was known as Henrik The Defender, Henrik Gornson spent many years as a boy living with and learning from magical fighting creatures all over the world. When he left home at a very early age, he was told that he had to make a choice. He could stay at home with his mother and sister, by the side of his father who was passing away, or he could give his life to the art of war, and in return, his father would be healed from a terrible sickness. He chose to save his father and sacrifice his own life, and it was at the age of thirteen, five years after leaving home, that Henrik met his first ninja.

There was a spirit that had walked with Henrik ever since he left home. It guided him. It called itself the Spirit of War, and it was the one who had healed Henrik's father from a sickness that doctors could not diagnose. The spirit had told Henrik in the woods, when he was eight years old, that it needed someone to defend human beings from the terror that was to come in future years, and that it was willing to give over part of its own energy to heal Henrik's father in return. The spirit had told Henrik that he was special, and that if Henrik continued with his training, then one day he would be powerful enough to heal people, just like the spirit could heal his father.

On Henrik's thirteenth birthday, he approached his family home through the woods. He could see the little house through the trees, and as he sat and watched, he saw his family walk outside. They stood there, on the grass, staring out at the forest. Henrik, at age thirteen, looked at least sixteen, and had developed a strong, muscular body and the beginnings of a thick beard. He wore a thin layer of dragon skin over his body that he had received as a gift a few years ago, and it kept him warm, even when it was cold. His brown hair was thick and his jawline was strong, and as he stared at his family in the distance, he sighed.

The Spirit of War was sat beside Henrik. It looked like a dark figure of a human being, covered in old but immaculate armour.

"You cannot return," the spirit said. "If you do, you will abandon your training through your desire to be with your family again. You have chosen your path. To return home will be breaking your promise to me, your father will become sick again, and I will not save him a second time."

Henrik had tears in his eyes. He wanted to at least say hello, to at least hug his mother. But the spirit said he couldn't, and it made him angry.

"Please," Henrik said. "Just for a few minutes."

"No," the spirit said. "No. You have made your choice, and now you must keep your promise to me."

Henrik thought of other creatures he had met recently who might be able to heal his father if needed. There was a friendly young dragon that Henrik had met when he was eight. The dragon had offered to help, but Henrik's family was so distrustful of dragons that they never let it in the house to do its work.

It was after the young dragon named Dengor was chased away by Henrik's mother who held a sword made from Garamanthium (which was poisonous to dragons of Dengor's kind). Henrik was then approached by the wondering Spirit of War, looking for the next great warrior to keep humanity safe from the evil and powerful creatures of the world.

Now, as he sat beside the Spirit of War, Henrik quietly looked up at the trees and said within himself:

"Please, send me some help. I wish to be with my family."

The Spirit of War stood and told Henrik that there was more training to do that day, and so Henrik stood, took one last look at his family, and walked off into the trees.

*

That night, when it was pitch black within the forest and Henrik was lying down to sleep, he felt something touch his foot.

Henrik quickly snapped awake, and went to grab the sword that he kept beneath his arm, but the sword was gone, and the small figure of a young girl wearing all black was crouching at his feet.

She quickly rose her finger to her mouth to indicate quiet, and despite Henrik's panic, he froze.

Henrik could see her eyes in the darkness. They were gleaming like an animal's would if it were to pass by a fire at night. The eyes shifted to look at the Spirit of War who was sitting beneath a tree nearby, also asleep. Henrik had always wondered why the spirit needed to sleep like a man, and the spirit's reply was always the same when Henrik would query it:

"Being awake and conscious in a world full of war is a terrible burden," the spirit would say. "Even I, as a spirit, need my rest from such a world."

Henrik had always wondered, every time the sprit said this, whether the spirit wanted a rest from the world around it, or a rest from the world built within its own mind.

Now, facing the young girl dressed in black, who also wore a dark face mask which only showed her glinting, shining blue eyes, Henrik heard her speak to him in his mind.

"This spirit beside you lives in fear," she said. "He has seen many battles and sees many more in his mind. If you want to be a real protector of people, you cannot fill your mind with violent thoughts. Otherwise, you end up trapped in fighting, just like this spirit."

Henrik looked and stared at the armoured spirit. He realised that even though the spirit could not be touched, it still wore armour as if it was vulnerable.

"I heard your call," the young girl said to Henrik. "You wish to see your family. I can help, but if this spirit finds out what you have done, its anger will be tremendous. Feeling betrayed, I do not know what it will do, to you or your family."

"I made a pact with the spirit," Henrik said. "When I was eight. I promised it that I would become dedicated to warfare if in return it healed my father."

"And are you still dedicated to warfare?" the girl asked.

"No," Henrik said. "But I am dedicated to protecting the people I love. I cannot put them at risk. If the spirit becomes angry, perhaps it will try to harm them. I cannot have that."

The young girl nodded.

"Perhaps I can still help," she said. "Wait until tomorrow."

"What will you do?" Henrik said, but as he asked the question, the young girl ducked away into the darkness, and she was gone.

*

"Wake up!" the Spirit of War said early the next morning. The sun was beginning to rise. "Your sword. Pick it up. It is time to train."

Henrik looked back to his side, and his sword was there again. He remembered the ninja from last night, and then quickly forgot her for a moment as the Spirit of War continued to harass him.

"Up! Up!" the spirit said. "This is no time for sleep!"

Every morning Henrik would fight the Spirit of War using his sword. The Spirit of War drew its own sword from a long scabbard at its waist, and for the purposes of training, the spirit's body would become solid. Whenever Henrik saw the spirit's armour beginning to glint, it meant that now the spirit could be touched as if it was still a man.

"What would happen to you if I managed to pierce through your armour when you become solid like this?" Henrik had asked once.

"Then I would die completely," the spirit said. "I would lose my form, become dissolved into the ethers, and the future of humanity would be doomed. Do not pierce through my armour. You may hit it. But do not pierce through any gaps if you see them."

Now, on this misty morning, while Henrik still felt sleepy as he stood to his feet, the glinting armour of the Spirit of War charged towards him. Henrik defended, he brought up his own sword and the spirit crashed into it as it swung its blade. Henrik had no armour, but the Spirit of War was very controlled. The worst that had ever happened to Henrik was a cut on his right shoulder.

"Your mind is elsewhere," the spirit said as it brought its armoured face down and close to Henrik's. "You are thinking about the past. What has happened?"

Henrik knew the spirit could sense that Henrik was thinking about something that happened in the night. He wasn't sure if he had dreamt it, but the eyes of that ninja now seemed to be etched in his mind.

"I'm still thinking about my family. I wish to see them," Henrik said.

"No!" the spirit said. "You must remember that you are humanity's only hope, Henrik." The spirit pushed Henrik away and Henrik stumbled back. "You aren't to see them! You will lose your allegiance to warfare, you will become soft again, a soft little boy! Your role in life is to become a warrior, to be so strong that you can take on entire armies of foul and ghoulish creatures all by yourself."

The spirit charged again at Henrik, and now Henrik felt fury start to bubble up from within him. He felt as if his life was in someone else's hands, and he felt frustrated that he did not have his own freedom. So, using his anger, he channeled it through his arms and through his sword, and this time, instead of defending an attack, he attacked the spirit as it charged towards him.

The spirit flinched for a moment, and before he could stop it, Henrik had swept the feet from underneath the armoured body, and was now standing over it, with his own sword hanging and dangling over the spirit's head.

"I don't like it," Henrik said. "I want my freedom."

The spirit felt fear within its own soul. Henrik had suddenly changed into something more ferocious.

"This is good..." the spirit said, slowly. "Very good. You are becoming strong, indeed, Henrik."

Henrik sheathed his sword, walked away amongst the trees, and left the Spirit of War on the ground, still holding its own sword.

*

The two of them continued to train that day. The spirit had Henrik running through the forest, lifting up small fallen tree trunks and climbing trees as quickly as he could.

"Faster! Faster!" the spirit yelled. "You are becoming so strong. You will be formidable in battle!"

Henrik jumped down from the top of a tall tree and landed in front of the armoured spirit. Its armour was no longer glinting.

"You are obsessed with battle," Henrik said, looking up at the armoured head that contained eyes that could not be seen.

"It is my role in life," the spirit said. "It is my purpose."

"Do you ever think that all of your thoughts about war actually attract it to you?" Henrik asked.

"Of course not!" the spirit yelled. "My thoughts have nothing to do with it. I am only doing what is right – training you so that you can protect future generations from harm."

Henrik kept looking up at the spirit.

"Couldn't you do it?" Henrik said. "Instead of me? Couldn't you fight whoever you need to, to keep future humans safe from harm?"

The spirit took a step back. Henrik could hear the birds singing, and suddenly he had more space.

"At the age of thirteen, you are already matching me for skill," the spirit said. "It is my aim to create the greatest warrior of all time, one who can protect anyone worthy of protecting. And you, dear Henrik, are he. Now, it is time for unarmed combat."

The spirit's armour glinted, it closed its armoured fist, and it stepped towards Henrik and swung a punch. Suddenly, and for the first time, Henrik could see the punch moving as if it was in slow motion. He seemed to have all the time in the world. He slowly ducked underneath the punch and moved to stand behind the spirit.

The spirit swung backwards, and once again Henrik ducked, then he picked up one of the feet of the spirit, drove him backwards and tripped the leg that he still stood on.

The spirit and his armour crashed into the base of a tree.

"Soon," the spirit said, "you will be ready for your first real fight."

*

That night Henrik could not sleep. He was expecting to see the ninja again, but as he waited for hours with his eyes open, looking around in the darkness, he began to lose hope.

"Maybe she'll never come back," Henrik said. "Maybe I really won't be able to see my family up close again."

And then, Henrik accidentally drifted off into sleep.

He was awoken by something nudging his right foot. He opened his eyes, went to grab his sword, but once again it was gone. The ninja girl was sitting at his feet, staring at him.

"They are here," she said. "I have brought them. Stand. Come with me. Silently!"

Henrik looked over towards the sleeping Spirit of War, in its usual position, lying up against the base of a large tree. Henrik could see clearly in the night, and it seemed to him that the spirit was asleep.

Henrik slowly and silently stood up, and the young ninja took his hand and led him away into the forest. Henrik could feel her gloved hand on his skin, and the feeling it gave him was unusual. It felt as if electricity was flowing out of her hand and up into his arm. It made him feel lighter than he had ever felt, as if he was almost floating along the forest floor.

After a few minutes of walking, in the distance Henrik could see a light. A flaming torch. As he walked closer, he saw that his father was holding it, and that beside his father stood his mother, and in front of them, his little sister.

Henrik wanted to run but the ninja turned and stopped him. She put her hand on his chest, and he slowed down again. Henrik got closer and could see his father's smiling face. His father was tall and slim with tough, leathery skin and a handsome look of pride that seemed to shine out of him. He always wore a buttoned-up shirt and black trousers. He didn't look as poor as he really was. Henrik's mother was wearing a floral dress, and she looked immaculately beautiful with her thick brown hair and beaming smile. And then there was Henrik's younger sister, Emelda, who was grinning at Henrik beneath her own brown curly hair and a dress that looked very similar to her mother's.

"Henrik!" his father whispered. Henrik walked up to his father and wrapped his arms around him. He felt that he could lift his father up if he wanted to.

"Goodness, you are getting stronger," his father said, finding it hard to breathe for a moment.

Henrik released him, hugged and kissed his mother, and then his younger sister, and then he looked at all of them.

"I'm sorry I had to go," Henrik said.

"We know...we know," his father said. "We have read your letters. We also read that you had to stop sending them to us."

"Yes," Henrik said, feeling guilty. "The spirit says my attachment to you must be gradually dissolved, so that I can fight freely without fear of death, but I..."

"Henrik," the young ninja suddenly said. "The spirit is coming."

Henrik quickly turned around, and through the trees he could see the dark, and now glinting form of the Spirit of War's armour, and he could feel the rage begin to reach him through the air.

"Henrik! We had an agreement! You are not to see your family! It is not right!" The Spirit of War started charging, and it drew its sword.

"They must not be allowed to distract you!" the spirit yelled, and as it charged, Henrik saw it change colour. The armour of the spirit turned red, the light began to glare off it, and suddenly Henrik realised its own anger was making it far more powerful than anything he had seen before.

"Henrik," the young ninja said. She threw Henrik his sword, and suddenly Henrik felt as if this Spirit of War was willing to kill his family, if it meant that Henrik had nothing left to focus on apart from the art of battle.

"Stop!" Henrik yelled. "Stop or I will fight you for real!"

"They must not be allowed here ever again!" the spirit yelled. "I must fulfil my purpose and train you to be a protector! It is important that..."

Then Henrik charged back at the spirit. He didn't even let him finish his sentence. The two collided in the middle of the forest, and Henrik's family could do nothing to help. Henrik's father ran towards the fighting pair, but the young ninja girl tripped him and held him down.

"You will be killed," she said to him, "do not go near."

"Henrik!" his mother yelled. She ran past the ninja and the ninja tripped her too, but Henrik's little sister, Emelda, ran past her mother and wanted to go and help her brother. Emelda was more fearless than anyone in that forest, and she believed she could help.

"Stop!" Emelda yelled, as her brown curly hair bounced as she ran. "Don't hurt my brother!"

The Spirit of War saw the little girl running towards them as it fought with Henrik, and the spirit pulled a metal dart from its waist. "I'm sorry, Henrik," it said. "The family is distracting us from our purpose together. This must be done." The Spirit of War broke away from Henrik for a moment and threw the dart at Henrik's sister.

Emelda saw the dart coming, and she ducked. It flew past her head and landed in a tree behind her.

As the spirit wondered how this girl's reflexes were so fast, Henrik swept the spirit again, placed his sword beneath the spirit's armoured helmet, and drove his sword up and into the spirit's head.

Knowing that he had lost, the spirit quickly became formless again before Henrik could hurt it. Its armour lost its hardness, and Henrik fell through its body.

"I cannot allow this to continue," the spirit said, rising to its feet. It ran towards the little girl, Emelda, and as it did, Henrik threw his own sword at the spirit's head in one last attempt to stop it. The spirit took form again, its armour glinted, and as it went to swipe through Emelda's body, she rolled underneath the sword, jumped up, clamped her hands around the spirit's helmet and ripped it off the spirit's head.

Underneath there was an old, scarred, reddened head, and as the spirit went to grab the girl, Henrik's sword landed, going straight through the spirit's neck, and the spirit fell, still with Emelda gripped onto its shoulders.

The spirit collapsed, and soon its entire body, including its armour dissolved, and Henrik felt as if a dark weight had been lifted off his shoulders.

Henrik heard a voice speak amongst the trees:

"Our pact has been broken, Henrik, and now I take back what I did. Your father will not live."

Henrik's father suddenly yelled and groaned in pain, and as Henrik and his sister walked up to him on the ground, his face looked old and yellow and gaunt, and he was clutching at his stomach.

"What has happened?" he said. "Henrik, what has happened?"

Henrik looked at the young ninja in front of him. She was glaring at him.

"There's only one creature who I know can help," Henrik said. "But you are going to have to trust a dragon."

Warrior

The warrior spirit lives within.

Henrik The Defender

Henrik The Defender was a noble warrior who was committed to keeping innocent people and creatures safe.

The next two chapters will continue Henrik's adventure, and you, young ninja, will be advised of some lessons about dealing with powerful creatures along the way...

95

Chapter 8 - Trusting A Dragon

"I don't know if I can accompany you," the young ninja said to Henrik as Henrik picked up his father over his shoulders. "I do not have a good history with dragons."

Henrik stared at the young ninja beside him, and she glared back at him in the way she usually did. Now Henrik's mother was holding the flaming torch, and Henrik's father felt limp and almost lifeless as Henrik carried him over his shoulder.

"Why not?" Henrik asked the young ninja. He stared at her for a while, and then he got the answer. It welled up in his chest.

"You have stolen from them before, haven't you?" Henrik said.

The ninja nodded. "But that was a long time ago," she said. "I wish I could fix things between me and the dragons."

Henrik began to walk off into the woods.

"Follow me," he said to his mother, sister and the young ninja. "This dragon is different. He is friendly, most of the time. Come with me if you want to know what a good dragon is like. And you will also have to tell me your name," Henrik said, as the young ninja followed after him.

The girl's name was Senyara. Henrik had many questions for her.

"How old are you?"

"I'm not allowed to say."

"Where do you come from?"

"I'm not allowed to say."

"How did you hear my call for help?"

"I'm not allowed to say."

Henrik walked a few more steps and laid his father at the base of a very special tree, that had a silver tinge on the bark.

"Well I'm grateful," Henrik said. "I'm grateful for you coming to help me, to bring me back together with my family, and also to free me from the Spirit of War."

"You're welcome," the young ninja Senyara said.

Henrik then lay flat on the ground, with his ear to the earth.

"He's under here. He's sleeping," Henrik said.

"Henrik," his mother said, still holding the flaming torch that illuminated her beautiful face. "Dragons can *never* be trusted."

"You're wrong, mother," Henrik said. "In my own experience, this dragon *can* be trusted." Henrik's sister, Emelda, was standing beside her mother, clinging to her leg, as if she had not just helped Henrik defeat and free the Spirit of War from its body. She looked like a normal little girl again.

"Dengor," Henrik whispered at the ground. "Dengor!"

Suddenly the ground rumbled, Henrik's body began to shake above the earth, and as if climbing out of bed, a small dragon, the size of a large man, quickly arose from the ground. The soil crumbled away from the dragon's body, and he clambered up out of the ground and stood there, with eyes still half-shut. The dragon was green, his body was thick, and there was an orange glow from the flames of Henrik's mother's torch shining on his scales.

"What? What do you want, Henrik?" the dragon said, yawning. Henrik knew that Dengor was always slightly irritable if woken up too early, and as he yawned, everyone saw how sharp Dengor's teeth were. They looked like finely carved knives.

"I'm sorry to wake you," Henrik said, "but my father, he's..."

The dragon named Dengor turned its handsome head to look at Henrik's father. Henrik's mother noticed how beautiful and intricate the scales were on its body, and now that it hadn't attacked any of them, she began to feel slightly calmer.

The dragon's face went from sleepy to concerned as it saw the sick man lying on the floor.

"He's sick again!" Dengor said, furrowing his browline. "How?"

"The Spirit of War took back its deed," Henrik said, "after I killed it for good."

The dragon smiled and looked at Henrik.

"So you are free? A free man?"

"He's just a boy!" Henrik's mother interrupted. The dragon snorted.

"You don't know anything!" the dragon laughed. Henrik always admired Dengor for his bluntness and honesty. "You were the one who chased me away with Garamanthium after I was about to help this man the first time!"

Dengor looked at Henrik, and regained his focus.

"Okay," Dengor said. "Here we go..."

Dengor took a huge deep breath in, and suddenly out of his mouth exploded a torrent of golden flames, and the golden flames covered Henrik's father.

"No!" Henrik's mother shouted. "No! Henrik, stop him!"

Henrik's mother went to run forward to stop the dragon, but Henrik met her, and held her still.

"Trust me," he said. "Dengor is a good dragon, he cares about people."

After a few moments the golden flames disappeared, and Henrik's father was beginning to stand to his feet. He didn't know where he was. He noticed the dragon beside him, and he began to run.

"Father!" Henrik yelled. "Wait!"

Henrik's father stopped, turned and saw his family, along with the young ninja and a small dragon standing in the forest, smiling at him, and suddenly he remembered what had happened that night.

"So you were right, Henrik," he said. "Some dragons *can* be trusted."

*

The next day, Henrik was in the forest again with the young ninja, Senyara, and the dragon named Dengor. Henrik's family were back at home and Henrik could see the cabin through the trees, now knowing he had the freedom to go back whenever he wanted.

"What will you do now?" Senyara said to Henrik. "Will you give up on your training? Will you give up on being a protector of people?"

Henrik looked back at his home. Now that he had his freedom back, he had an intense desire to continue developing his skills. He didn't need his family to survive anymore, he could take care of himself, and now there was a tremendous hunger within his heart to be able to defeat any creature in battle if he had to.

"I want to continue," Henrik said. "In many ways, the Spirit of War gave me a gift. He saw my talent and gave me a chance to develop my potential. I want to continue with the journey, and I want to train my sister to be even greater than she already is. I want to continue. But I'm not sure how."

Dengor the dragon was looking at the two of them. He had been speaking all night long with Senyara, and it had been concluded that while some dragons might never forgive her for what she did years ago, many others had forgiven and forgotten.

"You have to forgive yourself before you find real freedom," Dengor had said. "If you wait for all the dragons to forgive you, you might be waiting a long time before you can be happy."

Now the young ninja was looking at Henrik again. For the first time, her eyes looked teary.

"If you want to be a defender of people, then there is something I need help with," she said. "But it is not training. It is real life. It is dangerous. I cannot do it alone, and if I involve my own family, I will be risking their safety, putting them in danger."

Dengor snorted with interest and scraped one of his claws along the ground.

"What is it?" Henrik said, standing up straighter.

"It is my little brother. His name is Piyan. He has been taken by a terrible group of creatures known as the Nargans, and they are using him to try to make their own soldiers stronger. My little brother is special, his blood is valuable and powerful, and they managed to steal him away when he wandered too close to the forest's edge..."

Henrik could feel an overwhelming sense of duty and rage rise up in his chest. He thought of his own little sister. He felt something ancient flood his body that wanted to break through whatever was necessary to remove that innocent boy from evil hands. Before the ninja could finish her explanation, he said:

"I'll do it."

The ninja looked at Dengor, who smiled and blew out a short burst of blue flames from his nostrils.

"I have not been on an adventure in a while," Dengor smiled. He swiped his tail, stood to his feet and said: "I can fly us there, too. Let's go."

Friends

Challenges are easier alongside trusted friends.

Dengor The Great

Dengor is one of the few dragons that the ninjas trust without reservation. Even if a dragon claims to be Dengor The Great, do not trust it. Only Dengor The Great has scales that change from green to red when he is threatened or ready for a fight, so the only way to prove it is Dengor, is to speak to him about how he would feel if he was under attack right now. If this green dragon turns red, then it is indeed Dengor The Great. His story will continue in "The Ninja Chronicles Part 2".

Chapter 9 - The Ninjas And The Nargans

Before they left, Henrik, Senyara and Dengor gathered together in a small circle.

"Thank you," Senyara said, "thank you both. Before we leave, we must make a pact. You must promise me that you will not share my home with anybody else – you will never say where I or the other ninjas live. It must be kept a secret. Give me your hands."

Henrik placed his hand in the centre of the small circle. Dengor did the same with his own large clawed hand. As Henrik looked at the scales on the dragon's hand, it looked as if it would have taken someone hundreds of years to design such intricacy. Each green scale looked like a little shining universe, and in the centre of each scale, red was beginning to appear.

"This happens to me," Dengor said, looking at his scales changing colour. "If ever I am challenged to fight."

"We will not be fighting yet," Senyara said. "We will avoid it if we can." She placed her own hand on top of Dengor's hand. "Place your hand on top of mine, Henrik," she said.

Henrik did as she said, and he felt that same electricity almost lift him up off the floor again. Dengor smiled.

"Promise you will keep my home secret," she said to them both.

"I promise," Henrik said

"I promise," Dengor said.

Suddenly a burst of golden light shot out of Senyara's hand and flooded into both Henrik and Dengor's.

"Aggh!" Dengor shouted, and he jumped and backed away.

"The promise is sealed," Senyara said, "and now we will approach the Nargans, in secret."

*

Henrik had heard about the Nargans once before. He never liked the sound of them. The Spirit of War had told him about them once, years ago...

"Terrible creatures, are the Nargans, Henrik. They are thieves, parasites...the size of men, dressed in rags but with empty, soulless, ghoulish faces. Dark eyes and no noses – just open mouths where they breathe through. They are a distant relative of the

Marauders of Derdark, who I'm sure you will meet it in the future."

"What do they do?" Henrik had asked the Spirit of War.

"The Nargans steal creatures, mainly. Any creature they deem powerful – they steal it and harvest its energy. They will either sit around the creature, draining it of its mental energy, or they will drain its blood and attempt to place it within themselves. They don't usually eat food of any sort, but they do feed off creatures' life energy. Although..." the Spirit of War added, "they have been known to go mad for dragon meat. Even the smell of it makes them ferociously hungry."

"Henrik," the Spirit of War had said. "If you *ever* come across a Nargan, run away, and if you can't run, if you *must* fight, then don't look at any of them in their eyes. If you do, they can start to drain your energy before they even touch you."

"How can they be defeated?" Henrik had asked.

"Their bodies are weak," the Spirit of War had said. "Weaker than a man's. But it is vital that you never look them directly in their faces. Stay away from their eyes!"

Senyara was now climbing on top of Dengor's back, who had sat down on the ground. Henrik climbed up behind her and wrapped his legs around Dengor's body as tightly as he could to hold on.

"Hold on to my arms if you like," Senyara said. Henrik decided to cling to one of Dengor's spines instead, which was sticking up in front of where he sat.

"Ready?" Dengor asked, with Senyara's arms now wrapped around his neck.

"Ready. Fly east," Senyara said.

Dengor didn't move.

"Be more specific. I don't know what that means," Dengor said.

"Um...fly up and then that way," Senyara said, pointing with her fingers to the right.

"Right!" Dengor yelled, and he crouched down and exploded up into the air, opening his wings at his side and soaring up into the sky.

Henrik had never ridden Dengor before, or any dragon, for that matter. When he had first met Dengor, Dengor was very soft and tame, but over the years he had faced some challenges that had hardened his scales and sharpened his fighting abilities.

"How long will it take?" Henrik asked as they began to soar right, in the direction that Senyara had pointed.

"It depends how fast we fly!" Senyara yelled. Henrik could feel an intense whistling in his ears, and Senyara's long black hair was flowing down out of her headmask and into Henrik's face.

"I can fly fast, if you two hang on!" Dengor yelled.

Henrik looked over the side of Dengor's body and saw the trees beneath him. They looked extremely small, almost as if the life to him that seemed to be so important in that forest, actually meant nothing at all.

Henrik tightened his grip around Dengor's spine, and suddenly the whistling in his ears became more intense. He felt his body being pushed backwards, almost as if the air wanted Henrik to fly away from Dengor's body, but as Henrik held on tight and crouched down, resting his head on Senyara's back and gripping the dragon's body with his legs, Henrik felt them all plummeting across the sky as if they were all one arrow being fired out of a bow. He could hear Dengor laughing.

"I love to fly with a purpose!" Dengor yelled. His scales were gradually becoming redder, and Henrik felt his own instincts for battle begin to rise.

"Down there!" Senyara yelled, pointing towards an empty black hole that stood in between two forests. There was a field with this black hole in the middle. The hole looked small.

"The Escape Chasm!?" Dengor yelled. "Never! Who knows where we will end up? No one ever knows where that portal will take them! It's different every time! We could be thrown into the wrong land!"

"Not if we focus!" Senyara yelled. "It's the only way to reach my home. All of us, we have to stay focused on the forest to the left of my home village. We all have to say that we want to go to the Leyin Forest."

"What?" Dengor said, slowing down his flying and flapping his wings more slowly. "The what?"

"The *Leyin* Forest. From there we can sneak into the Nargan's fortress and save my brother. We don't want to go straight into my village. If my family sees me, they will try to stop me from saving my brother."

"Why?" Henrik said. He felt more at ease now that the flying had slowed down.

"My village fears the Nargans. They don't know how to defeat them. Everyone from my village who has ever seen a Nargan has fallen prey to it. No one else knows how to stop them."

"I do," Henrik said. "Don't look at their eyes. Don't look at their faces."

Senyara turned and looked back at him.

"I thought it was *fear* that we are supposed to avoid," she said. "I thought Nargans can only see you if you are afraid of death."

Henrik shrugged. "The Spirit of War told me not to look in their eyes. That's all he told me."

"Well I hope that's true," Senyara said, "because I still fear death. All of us, repeat: 'The Leyin Forest. The Leyin Forest. The Leyin Forest'."

Dengor was hesitant, but Henrik trusted Senyara. She had already helped him so much, and he wanted to help her in return. And now, strangely enough, Henrik felt as if he had the Spirit of War standing over his shoulder, but this time, instead of being the controller of his life, it was his useful guide.

"You will be ambushed," the spirit said to Henrik. Henrik wasn't sure if it was really the spirit, or just his own imagination.

"You will be ambushed," the spirit said again.

As Henrik repeated "The Leyin Forest. The Leyin Forest. The Leyin Forest" out loud, soon Dengor was repeating it too, and Dengor started to say it with such force that Henrik was sure he could sense a very unfamiliar smell – it smelt like trees that he had never met before. He was confused for a moment, but continued with the others to say "The Leyin Forest. The Leyin Forest. The Leyin Forest," and as Henrik felt he was *already in* the Leyin forest, although he had never visited before, Dengor turned his head down towards the escape chasm below them, the chasm that creatures saw as the absolute last resort to take if ever escaping from an enemy, and Dengor sharpened his body like a sword, pulled his wings back, pointed his head, and he ploughed down through the air, taking Henrik and Senyara with him, until the chasm grew larger in their sight, the darkness overtook them as they entered it, and they were being taken to a world that Henrik had never known.

*

The darkness disappeared, and the three companions were in a strange forest. The trees had frost clinging to all of them. It was cold. Henrik could feel the air biting at his face. The ground beneath them was hard, almost frozen solid, and as Henrik began to look around, he could see the misty air leaving his nose every time he breathed out.

"It's freezing," Henrik said, glad that he was covered in his dragon skin that kept him warm. "Senyara, is it always like this?"

"No," she said. Henrik looked at Senyara's eyes, and they looked concerned. They looked afraid and unsure. They began to dart around.

"Look out!" Dengor yelled, and just as he finished saying the words, Henrik instinctively ducked, and over his head came flying a large ninja, dressed in black, just like Senyara was, and its kick missed Henrik and it landed on the ground ahead of him. Henrik saw something running towards Dengor from behind, and as Henrik yelled, "Behind you!", a rope dropped down from the trees and wrapped itself around one of Dengor's hands on the forest floor. Dengor roared, his scales became redder than ever, and he breathed out hot fire that burnt the rope away. He turned, swung his tail, and the ninja that was running towards him from behind jumped over the tail, withdrew a dagger from its waist and tried to stab at Dengor's body.

Suddenly there was a huge fight. Masked ninjas were pouring in from everywhere, from above and behind trees, and they were all attacking Henrik and Dengor.

"Stop! Stop!" he could hear Senyara calling, but the intent of the ninjas to harm Henrik and Dengor was so strong that her voice was not doing much

113

good. Henrik had drawn his own sword, and he was ducking, fighting, kicking and tripping any ninja that came close. He could tell they were surprised by how well he could fight, and as he saw Dengor to the side of him, out of the corner of his eye, Dengor was burning the clothes off ninjas' bodies, swiping at their heads with his tail which had a spike on the end, and he was clawing at any of them that came close. Soon the ninjas had backed away, but they were throwing so many ropes at Dengor's body that he started to struggle to keep them all off him.

Henrik got kicked in the back of the head. He stumbled, he wobbled, he felt as if he could not control his feet for a moment, and then he heard the voice of the Spirit of War again in his mind.

"Show no mercy, now," the spirit said. Henrik had been holding back. He had been trying not to take any of the ninjas' heads off. But then his mind turned. He saw Dengor in trouble, and he decided to start destroying anyone who came close to him. Suddenly his sword flashed with bright white light, and every ninja in the forest turned and covered their eyes. This time Senyara yelled amidst the break and confusion, and her voice was louder than before.

"Everyone stop!" she bellowed. "These are my friends."

Henrik looked around. His sword was still shining so brightly that everyone except for him and Dengor had to keep their eyes closed.

"Everyone kneel down!" Senyara said. "If you don't, Henrik will start killing you!"

Slowly all of the ninjas began to kneel, Dengor burnt away the remaining ropes that were binding his body, and Henrik calmed down. His sword began to dim, and he looked at Senyara, who had been surrounded by five large ninjas.

"This...this is my family," Senyara said to Henrik. "They were trying to defend me."

Henrik slowly sheathed his sword and looked around at all of them. There were twelve ninjas, each on one knee, now looking at the ground.

"We are sorry," one of the large ninjas in front of Senyara said. "Senyara, we thought you were in danger."

The large man stood, turned, and embraced his daughter.

"Why is it so cold, father?" she asked.

"We thought it might help to keep any more Nargans at bay. We were told by a creature in this forest that they do not like the cold. We cast an ancient spell of frost."

115

The large masked man turned and looked at Henrik.

"Who is he?" the man asked.

"This is Henrik," Senyara said. "The dragon's name is Dengor. He is a friend. They both are."

Henrik could see the man's distrustful eyes glance toward the dragon. All of the ninjas were now staring at it.

"Don't look at me like that," Dengor said. "If I wanted to eat any of you, or steal your daughter away, I would have already done it. I'm here to help a boy who has been taken. That's it."

"I have a plan," Senyara said to her father, "but I didn't want to involve any of you."

"We have already lost two more men," her father said. "We tried to ambush the Nargans in our desperation to save your brother, but we could not break through, and now two more have been captured."

"Who?"

"Tenuki and Kenjo."

Senyara's eyes began to turn dark.

"Well, listen to my plan," she said. "I think it might work."

*

For a while, everyone sat together in the forest and listened to Senyara's plan. It was a simple one, but as Dengor listened to what she had planned for him, he began to speak up.

"Bait? You want to use me as bait?!" he said.

"It is a well-known fact that Nargans love dragon meat," Senyara said. "But because of my people's bad history with dragons, not many are ever seen in these woods. If they see you, Dengor, they will be compelled to hunt you down."

"So what am I supposed to do?" Dengor said. "Just run? You want me to just run away and not even turn to fight them?"

"If you turn to fight them," Senyara said, "you might fall under their spell. If what Henrik says is correct – you will not want to look at any of them in the eyes. If you fly away, they will probably give up, so you have to stay on the ground so that they chase you. We want them led away from their fortress. Are you a fast runner?"

"Yes," Dengor said. "But I've heard Nargans are faster than most creatures."

"They are," Senyara's father said, standing up and staring at the dragon. "They are faster than normal men. We struggled to escape them after we realised we could not fight our way through them."

"Why couldn't you?" Henrik said. "Why couldn't you fight through them?"

"There were so many. They would throw themselves before our eyes so that we were forced to look at them, and the feeling was strangely pleasurable...it felt euphoric, and yet many of us knew that if we were to become lost in the feeling, we would be sacrificing our very selves. Just two ninjas, Tenuki and Kenjo, got caught up in the allure of it all. They walked in deeper into the mass of Nargans ahead of us, and they were taken. They were the youngest of us who tried to save my son. Very strange. The Nargans are hideous, and yet to look at them in their eyes is pleasant."

Henrik now remembered something that the Spirit of War had been trying to teach him back at home, in the forest. It was part of Henrik's training that he had not completed.

"I am still here," he heard the voice of the Spirit of War say by his right ear. *"I told you that you would be ambushed. Your training can continue, but I see now that I do not have to hold you hostage for you to fulfil your destiny. You are doing it all by yourself. I am more powerful from this vantagepoint. I can see more, feel more. I am glad you freed me, and your sister is a real force to be*

reckoned with. I can help you, Henrik. I can allow you to see things without opening your eyes. Perhaps I can teach the ninjas too."

Henrik stood up as he made his announcement:

"I have a way of seeing without looking," Henrik said. "But it will take a bit of practice. If any of you wish to join me, then follow me."

Henrik turned from the group and began to instinctively wander off amongst the mass of cold, frosty trees that were behind him. Dengor stood and followed his friend, and one by one the ninjas followed him too.

*

Henrik led Dengor and the ninjas to a spot in the forest where it was warmer. The trees were not covered in any frost.

"For some reason the cold will not reach here," Senyara's big father said. It was difficult to tell the ninjas apart with only their eyes showing, but Henrik could see that Senyara's father had a different energy to the others – he was strong, but he was afraid.

"This is a power spot," Henrik said. "Some areas of forests cannot be affected by spells. They remain as they want to be, and in those areas, it is best to train."

119

The area that had not been touched by frost was small, but Henrik sat down in the centre. There were no trees, just bare ground with the tops of tree roots occasionally flowing out from it.

Henrik closed his eyes, and the ninjas watched.

"What are you doing?" Dengor said. "Should we be doing this too?"

Henrik could no longer hear Dengor. Sitting in this spot made his focus far more intense than it had ever been. He wanted to speak with the Spirit of War, and now he felt as if he was in an entirely different realm altogether.

Ahead of Henrik he could see the Spirit of War. Henrik was in a dark, empty space where there was barely any light, and the tall armoured figure of the spirit stood before him, motionless.

"Imagine that you can see with closed eyes," the Spirit of War said.

"But I can't," Henrik said. "Not yet."

"Just imagine it!" the Spirit of War yelled.

Henrik did his best. He closed his eyes and imagined himself being able to see his surroundings, even though his eyelids were shut.

"Okay," Henrik said. "Now what?"

"Keep doing it," the spirit said.

So Henrik did. He kept imagining that he could see with his eyes closed, until eventually, it began to feel real. He didn't know how, but gradually he began to believe that he actually *could* see without opening his eyes.

Suddenly Henrik felt himself back in the warm spot of the forest. He stood to his feet, but his eyes were still closed. Around him he could feel many beings. He could not see them as he would if his eyes were open, but he could feel the energy of every ninja and the one dragon that was standing in front of him. He could even feel the energy of some birds in the trees who had moved to this warm spot to be more comfortable.

"The cold is not needed," Henrik said out loud. "The Nargans do not mind the cold."

Henrik could feel disagreement amongst the ninjas.

"How do you know?" a voice said.

"I just do," Henrik said, still with his eyes closed. "Someone attack me. But do not injure me."

No one moved. They had seen how well Henrik could fight.

"I will not fight back," Henrik said. "I will only evade."

Henrik heard something moving towards him, and in his mind's eye he suddenly saw Dengor, red-scaled and feeling sneaky; Dengor moved to Henrik's right, and as he did, he swiped his tail at Henrik's legs. Henrik jumped, and the ninjas all gasped.

"His eyes are closed!" one of them said.

"Again," Henrik said. "More of you do it!"

Then more ninjas approached, some ran, some moved slowly, and they all tried to land a light punch or a kick somewhere on Henrik's body. But now Henrik knew what they were going to do even before they did, and just when it was necessary, Henrik would see what they were doing in his mind. His body would instinctively move up and down, forwards and backwards, deflecting more kicks and punches with his own arms and legs, and soon when the movements all stopped, he didn't even want to open his eyes.

"I can show you how to do this," Henrik said. "But you need to believe in your imagination."

*

After a while of teaching, the ninjas were struggling to have success. Henrik had guided them through a meditation where they would imagine themselves being able to see without vision, and when they would stand and face the test of Henrik reaching out to touch their necks, none of them were able to see him.

"I don't understand it," Henrik said. "It was easy for me to do it. The Spirit of War told me to just..."

"This is not part of our heritage," Senyara's father said, standing in front of Henrik and staring at him. "Perhaps we do not have the talent."

"Ah," Henrik said. "If you are assuming that you won't be able to do it because you have never done it before, then that is why you fail."

"Try me again," Senyara said. She was sitting at the base of a tree, and she stood to her feet. Her eyes were still closed.

Henrik walked through the other ninjas and stood in front of her. He waited. When he reached out to grab her neck, she grabbed his wrist.

The ninjas all gasped again.

"Let go," Henrik said. "Keep your eyes closed."

This time he waited a while longer, and Senyara raised her hand to grab Henrik's wrist, but Henrik had not moved.

"Don't try to guess," Henrik said. He waited another moment then reached out and wrapped his hand around her neck.

Senyara opened her eyes.

"I can't do it," Senyara said. "I can't do it!"

"But you did," Henrik said. "I think you just need more practice."

"We are running out of time!" Senyara's father said. "Henrik. We cannot spend much more time training. We have to act, we have to get our three ninjas out of there. My son is in there! They might drain him of his energy completely if we wait any longer. None of us can do what you do. You will just have to accept it."

"Henrik," Dengor said, sitting with his eyes closed under another tree, outside of the group of ninjas. "Try me."

*

Henrik had tested Dengor, and Dengor could do it. With his scaly eyes held shut, Henrik could swing his fists and kick his feet, and Dengor would swiftly evade every strike. Dengor could fight so beautifully, his movements were so smooth and fluid, and as he whipped his tail back at Henrik, Henrik had to evade as well.

"We should go," Senyara said. "At least you two can do it."

"What about all of you?" Henrik said.

"We will have to avoid their eyes as much as we can," Senyara's father said. "All of us did it before. We can do it again."

Henrik and Dengor stopped fighting as the big ninja kept speaking.

"Years ago the sight of a group of ninjas would have struck fear into the Nargans' hearts, but recently something has happened. They are losing their fear of us, and that is why some of them ventured out into this forest and stole my son. We have an old story in our tradition that states that the Nargans will always avoid ninjas. But now things are changing, and we don't know why."

"They used to take smaller creatures from forests far away," Senyara said, "to feed on their energy. But now they are taking people from nearby villages, and maybe they can sense even more power is within the ninjas."

Henrik closed his eyes. Now he could see every ninja around him as a glowing, golden figure of light.

"Let's go," Henrik said. "Let's go and save your people."

*

The walk through the icy cold forest was very quiet. Henrik noticed that all of the ninjas when walking, didn't make any sound at all. He tried to copy them, but he couldn't. His feet would crunch on the frozen leaves beneath his feet.

"How do you do it?" Henrik asked Senyara, who was walking ahead of him.

"What?" she whispered back.

"Move so quietly."

"Practice," she said. "It's just practice. Now be quiet, we are drawing near their fortress."

After an hour of walking through the woods, with Dengor at the back of the group, who would occasionally breathe flames over his own body to warm himself up, the group of thirteen ninjas, Henrik and the dragon could see in the distance there was a clearing, and in the clearing was a large wooden fortress with a gang of Nargans standing outside of the front gate.

The Nargans stood motionless. Henrik could see their empty mouths, their soulless faces, and something within him wanted to keep looking.

"Be careful, Henrik!" Senyara's father hissed. "This is how it begins. Do not look at their faces!"

Henrik felt as if he wanted to get up from behind the tree that he was hiding behind and walk towards the Nargans so he could get a closer look.

His leg twitched, and Senyara punched him in his calf muscle. Henrik snapped out of it and looked at her. Her eyes were icy blue.

"Stop!" she said. "Use your powers now. Close your eyes."

Henrik looked behind himself and saw Dengor nod, and his scaly eyes close. Henrik did the same. Now, strangely enough, Henrik could see more clearly than before. The ninjas around him were no longer golden shapes. They looked like ninjas. The trees looked similar, except there was a white light travelling through all of them. With his eyes now shut, Henrik looked towards the Nargans, and while he could see their grey bodies and brown rags for clothes, he could not see their faces.

Senyara turned to look at Dengor, and she nodded at the dragon.

Dengor rose to his feet and began to walk slowly, with his eyes closed, through the trees and towards the Nargans.

"Good luck, everyone," he said, and as he walked out of the trees and into the clearing, the Nargans saw him, and they began to point and scream.

It was a foul language that made Henrik's insides squirm, and suddenly the screaming grew louder, and the Nargans standing outside of the fortress began to charge at Dengor.

Dengor took a deep breath in and blew such a ferocious breath of fire out of his lungs that it engulfed the group of Nargans, and it burnt them all to a crisp.

When Dengor's breath of fire ended, there were just black ashes on the ground in front of the fortress.

The gate opened ahead of him, and a huge group of Nargans poured out and began to run towards Dengor. Dengor didn't move.

"What's he doing?!" Senyara said. "He was supposed to draw them away! I didn't know a dragon so small could breathe fire like that!"

"He practices a lot," Henrik said. "And he learnt from the best."

The Nargans, running through the gateway of the fortress that acted as a funnel were suddenly faced with such ferocious flames, that they too were beginning to burn to ashes. It was only when the Nargans stopped, realising that they would die if they were to walk through that fire, that Dengor stopped too. He started to cough. His fiery breath turned blue and cold, and he started to clutch at his own chest as he reared up on his hind legs.

The Nargans saw the dragon struggling, and holding their spears and knives and swords, they could not help themselves from hunting down a weakened dragon. A dragon's meat was so nutritious to them, that this one would be able to sustain them for years.

Dengor looked back towards the group of ninjas and smiled.

"I had to burn some," he said, winking one scaly eye at Henrik. "And I will burn all of those who chase me."

Dengor continued to pretend. He keeled over and acted as if something had just exploded inside his chest. The big group of hungry, salivating Nargans charged out of their gateway and towards the dragon who they were expecting to pounce on and kill, and just as they arrived, Dengor rose to his feet and ran off to the left. Henrik and the ninjas watched as most of the population of Nargans, going mad with the smell of dragon meat, all poured out of their homes holding their weapons and chased after the dragon into the depths of the woods. After a while the outpouring of Nargans ended, and Henrik led the ninjas towards the gates of the fortress.

With his eyes closed, it was as if Henrik could see through walls. He could see the remaining Nargans within the fortress, before he had even reached the gate.

"I can see them," Henrik said. "I can see all of them."

He began to run straight ahead, the ninjas followed, and then they all heard the Nargans start to scream as Dengor burnt them all away in the forest he had led them in to.

*

Henrik was keeping his eyes closed. As he led the group of ninjas in through the main gates, he could see around him little wooden huts, and within each hut he could see a grey shining outline of a Nargan.

"Which way, Henrik?" Senyara asked as Henrik slowed down and looked around.

"To the centre," Henrik said. "We have to walk past these huts and make it to the centre of the fortress."

Henrik moved as quietly as he could. He led ninjas around different huts, creeping low to avoid being seen through windows, and if ever a Nargan was moving from inside their hut to outside, Henrik would know. He would hear them. A little alarm seemed to ring in his mind, and as he would turn in the direction of the moving Nargan, through the misty walls of huts in his vision, he could see where they were moving. After a while of creeping and sometimes running across gaps in between huts, the group arrived at a large building in the centre of the fortress. This one was not made of wood. It was made of stone, and Henrik could not see so easily through the walls.

"They are in there," Henrik said, "I can not see them. But I can feel them."

"Me too," Senyara said. "I don't think they know anything about Dengor approaching their fortress. The walls look too thick to allow any sound inside."

Henrik began to lead the group of ninjas again. He ran towards the enclosure, and just as he did, the stone door opened.

Henrik had not been able to sense it, but as the door opened and a Nargan walked out, Senyara threw a dart straight at its head. The dart pierced through the Nargan's face, and it fell to the ground in a slump.

Henrik looked back at Senyara for a moment. She had been sure to only look at the Nargan's face to aim for a second. Now she was looking at the base of the building ahead of them.

Henrik crept up to the fallen Nargan, and he dragged the body out of the doorway. It smelt awful. The odour was of acidic, burning metal, and Henrik suspected it was coming from the blood of the Nargan that was gradually leaving its face.

"We don't have much time," Henrik said. "If the smell spreads, soon they will all know about it. Come on."

Henrik led the ninjas inside the stone building, and suddenly he could hear screams.

*

"Never! Never!" Henrik heard a man shouting. The inside of this building was dark. Henrik could feel the stone of the walls with his hands. It was uneven and rough, and as he walked carefully but swiftly through these dark corridors, he stopped again. They had reached a ledge, and Henrik, still with closed eyes, was able to see over the ledge and look down, where there was a young boy lying on a stone, not moving, and either side of him were two ninjas in small cages, also standing on large stones.

"We will never give you our power!" one of the ninjas yelled. Both of the ninjas in cages had closed their eyes. Something must have happened that made them stop wanting to look the Nargans in the faces.

"Open your eyes!" a Nargan yelled. There was a group of ten Nargans standing before the three ninjas on stones, and they were all staring at the ninja who kept shouting. He stood on the left.

"That's Tenuki," Senyara whispered to Henrik. This ninja was large and round, with a permanent scowl on his big face. His mask had been removed, and he had remarkably shiny thick hair.

"No!" Tenuki yelled back at the Nargan. "We fell for that once, until we noticed what you had done to young Piyan beside us. He is just a child! How could you do it? Stole him from right beside his own village, didn't you!"

"The boy has been drained of energy. He is recharging on that Earthstone," the same Nargan said. "He has been helping strengthen our own soldiers, who stand on guard against intruders and hunt any dragons that come across our path. Now we must feed off *your* energy. Open your eyes. It will feel good."

"No!"

"*Open your eyes,*" the Nargan repeated.

"No!" Tenuki yelled. "We should never have succumbed to you in the first place! We were weak." He looked at the young boy beside him again, Senyara's younger brother, Piyan. "That boy has a family! And yet you plan to keep him here as your prisoner? You will pay, mark my words, you nasty beasts! You will pay!"

The ninja in the cage on the other side of the child was very quiet and still.

One of the Nargans walked up to Tenuki, holding a sword that had been sitting in the embers of a fire nearby. There were fires dotted all around the room, which to Henrik looked more like a cave.

The Nargan walked up the five stone steps in front of Tenuki, where Tenuki's little cage was, and the Nargan thrust the sword into Tenuki's stomach.

Tenuki felt the burning, searing pain of that sword enter his flesh, and his cage was so small he was not able to move away.

"Agghh!" Tenuki screamed, but as he did, he grabbed hold of the Nargan's hand who was wielding the sword, and Tenuki snapped one of its fingers off. Now the Nargan screamed, it dropped the sword in the cage, and Tenuki pulled the Nargan in towards him so fast that the Nargan's face and body cracked against the bars of the cage, and something in the structure began to weaken. The Nargan's body went limp, and Tenuki looked down, now opening his eyes and reaching for the sword.

He picked it up and tried to cut through the bars with this glowing, red-hot sword, and just as he was managing to break through the first bar that had been weakened by the Nargan's head, the rest of the Nargans had withdrawn their own swords, and were running up the stone steps to stop him.

"Now!" Henrik whispered, seeing that all the Nargans were distracted.

Henrik ran out on to the ledge and climbed down the stone wall in front of him as if he was an ape. Senyara took a ninja rope from her back, wrapped it around a jagged edge of the ledge, and she descended down the rope to the ground beneath.

The other ninjas followed, and soon Henrik was withdrawing his own sword and running towards the Nargans who were attacking Tenuki.

Then there was a fight. Henrik cut and stabbed and sliced through Nargans' bodies until they were trying to grab at his face to open his eyes, and all the while, ninjas behind him were throwing their darts at Nargans and causing them to fall.

"Stay away!" Henrik yelled to the ninjas, freeing himself from hands and battling with Nargan swords until only one of the creatures was left. It was standing in front of Tenuki's cage, and Henrik could sense that Tenuki was now bleeding.

"Do not destroy me," the final Nargan said. Henrik didn't like the voice at all. There was something very odd and sickly about it. Henrik still had his eyes shut and could see the grey outline of the Nargan's body starting to become dark. Then the Nargan said something else:

"If you decide to kill me, it is decreed that you will awaken a force far greater than us Nargans," it said. "I am the leader, but our sleeping ancestor is so great that it will not tolerate..."

Then Henrik saw the big strong arms of Tenuki wrap themselves around the Nargan's neck from the cage behind, and squeeze so hard that the Nargan quickly stopped breathing.

"Free them, and run," Henrik heard another voice say. It was the Spirit of War. Henrik could see it over by one of the fires, pointing at the embers. *"Place your sword within the embers, free these ninjas, and then run."*

"Run?" Henrik said. "From what?"

And then from under the stony ground beneath Henrik's feet, Henrik heard something roar so loudly that his feet and legs began to vibrate.

"Hurry," the Spirit of War said. *"And carry the boy!"*

*

The ground started shaking as if it was about to explode. Henrik opened his eyes, ran over to a fire behind Tenuki's cage, and he stuck his sword inside the embers. After a few seconds the sword was glowing with orange, and while Henrik looked towards the ninjas who were looking around waiting for something to attack them, Henrik took his sword, walked up to Tenuki's cage and began to swipe at the metal bars. He swiped, then hacked, and gradually he began to cut through the bars and make an opening for Tenuki to squeeze through.

"What is happening!?" Tenuki yelled. The rumbling in the ground was becoming louder. "What's about to happen?"

"Run!" Henrik yelled. "Carry out the boy and take the ninjas with you!"

Tenuki, after squeezing out of the cage, quickly thanked Henrik, ran to Senyara's brother, who still looked asleep on the rock that he was on, picked him up and began to run away towards the other ninjas. Henrik ran to the other cage, where the final ninja named Kenjo was standing, now with his eyes open.

"I knew you would come," Kenjo said over the rumbling. "Thank you, Henrik."

Henrik didn't know how this ninja knew his name, but as soon as he hacked through the metal bars of the cage, Kenjo was freed, and together with Henrik he climbed the wall at the back of the cave using the ninja rope that still hung there, and they began to sprint through the dark stony corridors and out of the building.

Then they were met with more Nargans, the remaining ones who had moved out of their homes.

"The Nenarla awakens, the Nenarla awakens," they all began to chant, and while they didn't attack any of the ninjas, they stared, and stood back, as if something far greater than them was about to do something for them.

Henrik closed his eyes again to avoid looking at any of them, and then suddenly, with his eyes once again closed, he could sense what was about to happen. Something was moving underground, planning to meet him and the ninjas where they exited the fortress.

"Wait!" Henrik yelled at the ninjas who were sprinting off ahead of him. All of them were looking at the ground, sprinting between Nargan huts and hurrying towards the gates of the fortress. "It's a trap!" Henrik yelled. "There is something waiting for us there!"

"We must get out of here!" Senyara's father called back, and as they continued to sprint, as Henrik and Kenjo followed behind, the ninjas made it to the gates of the fortress, and just outside of the gates, the ground exploded.

Out of the ground rose an enormous figure. It looked like a giant Nargan, but it began to scream so loudly that Henrik and all the ninjas had to cover their ears.

"It's too loud!" Henrik managed to hear Kenjo scream beside him. His voice was muffled. "It's too much!"

The pain was intense, Henrik felt as if his own ears were about to burst, and just as Henrik felt his entire mind begin to turn fuzzy, and just as he had an overwhelming desire to look up at the giant Nargan, as if looking at it with open eyes would end the terrible screaming, Henrik heard something else begin to roar.

He knew it was Dengor, and as Henrik looked through closed eyelids at the skinny legs of the giant Nargan that were taller than the trees behind it, Dengor's flames engulfed its knees, and the giant began to buckle.

"Keep running!" Dengor yelled at all of the ninjas. The screaming stopped for a moment, and the Nargan had to plant a large, sinewy hand on the ground. Dengor fired flames at the hand with such intensity that the hand began to dissolve, and as the Nargan tried to stand to its feet again, the group of ninjas ran around it and into the forest. Henrik followed, with Kenjo by his side, until he ended up behind the giant, and Henrik withdrew his sword.

He sprinted at the Nargan's ankles and began to cut. The Nargan yelled, but it no longer had the energy to scream. Dengor had taken flight, and with his own scaly eyelids tightly shut, he flew directly at the Nargan's face and breathed out so much fire that the Nargan yelled and stumbled back. As it stumbled its ankles would no longer support it after Henrik had been cutting, and when it fell back into the trees it made such a crash that Henrik was lifted off the ground for a moment.

The remaining Nargans began to run out of their fortress and towards Henrik, outraged at what was happening, and as Henrik fought with them, Dengor began to scratch and cut and burn away at the giant's throat, until the giant stopped yelling, and all of its struggling stopped.

Henrik dealt with the remaining Nargans with ease. A few were left to run away, and Henrik turned, looked at the fallen giant and saw Dengor standing on top of it.

"Well," Dengor said. "That was fun."

*

After Henrik and Dengor caught up with the ninjas in the forest, they were reviving Senyara's younger brother. All of the ninjas were kneeling around him, chanting something so beautiful that Henrik's eyes began to well up. Very gradually the boy lying in the middle of the circle of ninjas began to awake, and he looked around with a slight smile.

"I had a dream," he said. "A dream that I was taken."

"And now it is over," Senyara's father said. "Now it is all over."

Then the boy was led out of the circle, and the large ninja, Tenuki, collapsed in his place. His clothes were torn and his body and face were cut and bleeding from the Nargan swords. As the ninjas chanted for him, in a sharper, faster tone, soon Tenuki's cuts were healing, and he was standing to his feet.

Senyara's father stood as well, followed by his daughter, and they approached Henrik and Dengor. All the other ninjas rose to their feet, and as they turned to face Henrik and the dragon, they all bowed.

"Thank you," they all said together. "Thank you, Henrik. Thank you, Dengor."

Henrik and Dengor bowed back.

"Our pleasure," Henrik said, feeling such an overwhelming sense of satisfaction in his heart, such a strong sense of victory seeing the boy and the two other ninjas returned to their group, that Henrik felt as if he would not be able to sleep for days. The feeling of joy within him was too strong. This was what he was supposed to do. This was how he was supposed to spend his life, defending the innocent from forces of evil, and as he stood up straight again, with his friend Dengor by his side, he looked up and saw the Spirit of War sitting in a tree, and although Henrik could not see the spirit's face, he knew it was smiling.

"And now," the spirit said. *"Your real life begins."*

Talent

Use your talents and abilities to your advantage.

Never Trust A Nargan

Never trust a Nargan,
whatever form they take.
Sometimes they dress as humans in disguise.

They move through trees in silence
and if you are not ready,
they'll draw you in to stare you in the eyes.

And if you meet their gaze,
you could be there for days,

they'll feed upon your ninja strength and power.

But if you look elsewhere,
with disciplined attention,
then your energy they won't devour.

Keep your focus on their bellies,
do not think to waver,
then you can fight with freedom, without fear.

But if temptation takes you
and you look them in the eyes,
then into hands of darkness, you will steer.

To join Henrik on more adventures as he fights to protect innocent kingdoms from evil forces, TURN TO PAGE 192...

Chapter 10 - Senyara And The Dragons

When Senyara was five years old, she was revered by all the ninjas in her village as a very talented girl. Before she had even begun to train, she could sneak up on the other ninjas in the village without even trying. They might have been working in the fields growing crops, washing clothes or preparing food, and all of a sudden they would feel a tap on their legs. They would turn around, and Senyara would be standing there, looking up into their eyes, making them wonder how their highly tuned ninja senses had not been able to detect a young girl walking up behind them.

"I have never seen anything like it," a ninja named Yenza said to Senyara's father as they stood in a field of big beautiful crops. "She moves like the air. None of us can sense her coming, not by sound nor by intention. It's as if she has a natural cloaking device. She will grow to be a tremendous ninja, indeed."

It was when Senyara was six, after one year of ninja training, that something terrible happened to her village.

The people she was raised by only wore black clothing and masks if they planned to move stealthily through the woods or other areas where there were shadows. In their day-to-day lives they all appeared as a normal community of people, closely-knit and working together to provide a life for themselves, living off their own land and drinking from the streams in the woodland nearby.

But when this terrible thing happened, even this secretly trained community of ninjas were not able to stop some of the destruction that was heading their way.

There were gangs of creatures who lived in the swamps to the east. These creatures were called Gangraiders. They were small grey vicious creatures about the size of children, but they carried sharp weapons. Some of them wore old beaten armour that they had found discarded in the woods over the years, and they could fight with speed and viciousness. If they ever tried to invade Senyara's village, they were usually swiftly beaten, kicked or assailed by an onslaught of ninja stars into their necks, but recently they had recruited the services of a much more terrible creature.

They had recruited a Cropmuncher. It was a wide, armoured beast that stood the height of two men. Its skin was brown but so tremendously thick that it had been said that no man-made weapon could pierce through it. Its eyes were tiny in a head that was thick, rhino-like and armour-plated, and this creature was said to only awaken once every seven hundred years.

Unless it was awoken on purpose.

The Gangraiders believed that Senyara's village might have treasure hidden somewhere beneath their little cabins made from wood. They did not. Senyara's community barely had any money, and were completely dependent on their crops for survival. So when the Cropmuncher was seen to come wading out of the trees in the distance, hungry and desirous to eat any crops of the ninjas it could find, the ninjas all focused on the creature, and did everything they could to stop it wading through their fields and quickly eating everything they had worked so hard to grow that summer.

In the heat of the day, Senyara heard one of her people shout:

"It's...I think it's a Cropmuncher. Everyone, come, we must fight!"

And fight they did. They fought with everything they had, but the Cropmuncher's armoured legs, face and body were so strong that they could do nothing to stop it. It was so strong that they could not hold it with ropes, and as it waded through their fields, eating everything in sight, Senyara was standing off to the side behind her father.

"Stay there, Senyara! You are the youngest amongst us! Do not go to where the Gangraiders are!" her father yelled.

Senyara watched this huge armoured creature snort and scream as an entire community of ninjas tried to cut or stab or tie it up, and she looked over to the cabins to the left, where the Gangraiders were rushing through each building, trying to find any treasure they could. Senyara saw one of them carrying her mother's dress, and Senyara suddenly felt furious.

She disobeyed her father. She had her own set of daggers that she had been trained to use, and a little sword at her waist that she had been practicing with for six months. She withdrew the sword, and while the Gangraiders were inside the cabins, seeking frantically to find anything of value, Senyara began to attack them. She was strangely insensitive to blood, and the fury she felt deep within her towards these little nasty creatures trying to take what belonged to her people meant that she started killing Gangraiders as quickly as she could. She ran between cabins, slaughtering them without any sense of mercy, and since she was so quiet, none of the Gangraiders knew what was happening. By the time she had snuck up on a group of them, they barely had any time to react, and if any of them did decide to fight her, Senyara's skills with her sword were already so great that she made it all look easy. She pinned one of them up against a wall of her own cabin, with her sword to its throat, and she asked it a question.

Its face was snarling and vicious, with teeth like little daggers, and as she leant her sword into its neck, she asked:

"What are you looking for?"

"Treasure!" the Gangraider spluttered. It could feel the blade beginning to seep into its own neck. "Treasure. That's all we want. All we want is your treasure, nothing more!"

Senyara looked around. "We don't have any," she said. "Why do you want treasure?"

"To buy things with!" the Gangraider spluttered again. "There is barely any food growing by our swamp, and we have to buy things from other creatures. We can't stand what you grow on your land. Horrible, it is." More of its friends were still outside searching anywhere they could. "Barely anyone's got any treasure anymore. Most of it belongs to Hades the dragon!"

Senyara cut the creature's throat, ran out of her cabin and chased down every Gangraider she could, before just one was left, and the rest were fleeing with nothing in their hands.

"Why don't you steal from Hades the dragon?" she said. "If he's got all the treasure, why not raid him instead?"

The last creature was fearful. It was pinned down on the ground by Senyara and its wide mouth was grimacing.

"Don't kill me," it said. "Please. If I tell you things, will you promise not to kill me?"

Senyara nodded, knowing that day one of her ninja training was all about deception, of never needing to tell the truth to an enemy.

"We tried, once," the Gangraider winced. "The dragon started to eat us. It came to our swamp and stole everything we had worked so hard to gather for ourselves."

"You mean everything you *stole*?" Senyara said.

The creature nodded. "It is very unwise to ever steal from a dragon. And he is friends with other dragons. He has brothers and sisters that are even worse than he is. We...we need money so that we can..."

"Where is the dragon!?" Senyara yelled. "Your monster is eating all of our food in our fields, so now *we* will need treasure so that we can buy some from another village. Where is the dragon?"

The Gangraider began to laugh.

"Ten miles north. It lives beneath the Underway Hill. But you are only a girl."

"One last question..." Senyara said, gritting her teeth and pressing her blade deeper into the Gangraider's throat. "If you want to save your own life, tell me how that monster in our field can be defeated."

The Gangraider couldn't help but smile again. "Only when it's had enough to eat, will it return to its home. We needed it as a distraction. It is an indestructible creature."

Senyara looked back at the fields where the creature was just about finished eating everything that her people had grown over recent months.

"Now will you let me go?" the Gangraider asked beneath Senyara's blade.

"No," Senyara said. "You will come with me."

*

Feeling that her village was soon to be without any food, and knowing that they barely had any money between them, Senyara was sure that it was now up to her to obtain treasure so that her people could buy food to survive. She had a memory in her mind of her father from the year before, as she began her ninja training at the age of five...

"Senyara," he said. "Our crop fields are everything to us. We must always do everything we can to protect them if they come under attack. Our village

152

is poor, and jobs are very scarce in other villages. We are not rich with money, but we are rich with land, and we intend to keep it that way."

Senyara had seen her father do some amazing things. He had healed people with his bare hands, he had defeated dozens of men at once who came one night to steal food. He could even affect the weather if he was left alone for a few hours in deep meditation, and yet, she thought it strange, that he could not use his powers to attract money.

"It is not good to have lots of money," he had said to her once. "Rich people are usually immoral and exploitative, making people work all kinds of hours so that they themselves become rich."

"But, father," Senyara said, "is that really true?" She could imagine her father as a rich man, and when she did, he was not immoral. He was grand and wise and wealthy, like a benevolent king. "Couldn't riches be in the hands of good people too – just like there are good poor people and bad poor people, couldn't there be good rich people too?"

Her father screwed up his face, as if his five-year old daughter was poking something painful inside of him – poking at the false beliefs he had built that had accidentally prevented his own wealth.

"Enough of this, Senyara" he said. "Now let us begin your training."

Now as Senyara heard the shouts of ninjas and the bellows of the Cropmuncher, she wrote a note addressed to her father and left it on his bed in their cabin. Then she began to walk out of her village and towards the forest beyond it, knowing that what she planned to do was wrong. She knew her father would never let her leave the village by herself, let alone go to steal from a terrible dragon.

She justified it to herself in her mind by saying that the dragon deserved it. It was a thief. Surely there was nothing wrong with stealing from a thief. If this dragon had stolen so much treasure from so many creatures, the amount that Senyara planned to take, in comparison, was very small.

She was dragging the Gangraider along behind her, her small fingers clamped around one of its big grey ears.

"Let me go!" the Gangraider said. "Let me go or I will bite you!"

"If you bite me," she said, "then I will cut off your legs."

The Gangraider went quiet, and Senyara took one last look back at her village, where she could see all of her people still clambering, shouting and fighting, trying to stop the Cropmuncher from eating their last remaining pieces of food.

*

Senyara disappeared off into the trees, and her father suddenly felt something lurch inside his stomach. He turned around after narrowly avoiding being cut in half by the one long horn on the end of the Cropmuncher's head.

"Senyara! Senyara!" he called. As he called out, frantically looking around for his daughter, another thought flashed into his mind.

One small corner of crops remained in the field, and Senyara's father knew of an ancient way that might be able to save this year's harvest. There was a creature in the forest who could replicate crops, but it was rarely ever seen, and asked much in return for its services.

Then Senyara's father had another idea. He noticed that the Cropmuncher's eyes were tiny, kept safe behind a thick mound of hard, armoured flesh, and that as it moved and swiped its head sideways to bat away ninjas as it ate, kicking its rear legs as much as it could to keep the ninjas off it, it was snorting at the ground tremendously loudly.

Senyara's father had a pocketful of Sticky Herb that he always carried around in case of an emergency. Sticky Herb could be placed on the skin of anyone who was injured in the crop fields, and after he said a blessing over it, their cuts would begin to heal. But Sticky Herb was pungent. The smell was so strong that even to be near it would sting the insides of people's nostrils. He held his breath and took the Sticky Herb out of his pocket, in a big sticky ball of green leaves and thin vines. He broke the ball in half, and as his eyes began to sting and tear-up from the smell, he ran up to the Cropmuncher, avoiding another swipe of the horn, and he stuck one of the balls of herb inside one of the Cropmuncher's large nostrils. The Cropmuncher snorted and reared up on its hind legs, and before Senyara's father could fill the other nostril, the Cropmuncher began to spin around in circles, throwing its head up and down, still snorting, trying to get the Sticky Herb out of its airway, but making it continually worse. It started thrashing around, and the ninjas backed away.

"Aim for the mouth!" Senyara's father yelled, "but from over there!"

Senyara's father pointed in the direction of the broken fence that the Cropmuncher had crashed through, that led away into a broken path in the forest that the Cropmuncher had also created. He and the other ninjas ran towards the fallen fence, turned, and as the Cropmuncher was facing them with an open mouth, trying to get extra air into its lungs, the ninjas threw their metal, razor-edged stars so that they entered and sometimes hit the Cropmuncher's tongue.

The Cropmuncher screamed again and faced in their direction. Still facing them with an open mouth, no longer facing down at the ground to eat, more ninja stars were thrown into the monster's mouth, and as more blades cut into the insides of its mouth and throat, the angry monster charged straight in their direction.

"And now," Senyara's father said, "everyone lead it to the Northern Cliff. I have to find my daughter!"

*

Senyara led the Gangraider away further into the forest, and she let go of its ear.

"Thanks," it said, gruffly, rubbing its own ear. Senyara had left fingerprints in the Gangraider's floppy ear from where she was squeezing so hard.

"There's no way I'm going to help you steal something from Hades the dragon!" the Gangraider hissed.

Senyara looked around. She had never been allowed in this forest by herself before. It was beautiful. Birds were singing gently, and sunlight filtered in through the trees and illuminated the brown leaves on the forest floor.

"I hate the forest," the Gangraider said. Senyara inspected the creature for a moment. The rags it wore around its waist were old and tattered. It had a skinny, wiry grey body and an oversized head with no hair. It looked like a distant relative of a goblin, and when it walked it swayed from side to side.

It no longer had any weapons, since Senyara took its little knives away back at the village.

"How long will you keep me with you?" it said to her, kicking its feet across the ground as it walked.

"Just take me to the lair of the dragon," she said. "Then I will let you go."

"What if we get ambushed?" the Gangraider said. "There's creatures here that will probably have us for their dinner! Especially with me not being armed."

"The faster you take me there, the faster you can leave and go home," Senyara said.

"Fine," the Gangraider said, sniffing. "Try to keep up, will you."

Senyara nodded, and the Gangraider suddenly bolted away into the depths of the trees.

*

Senyara had been sprinting for a while, and she was growing tired.

"Hurry up!" the Gangraider yelled. "Don't slow down, little girl, or you will lose me!"

The Gangraider was beginning to get away from her. Its little body was starting to become even smaller in front of her as the distance between them grew.

"Stop!" she said. "Wait! Slow down." The Gangraider turned and flashed a menacing smile at her with its big sharp teeth, and if anything, it began to speed up.

"Wait!" Senyara said. "Wait!"

Just as the Gangraider was beginning to taste the freedom that lay ahead of him, Senyara took a dagger from her waist and threw it directly into the back of one of the Gangraider's shoulders.

The Gangraider yelped, tumbled, rolled for a while, and hit the base of a tree.

Senyara ran up to it and removed the dagger. It had not gone too deep.

"Why did you do that?!" the Gangraider yelled, clutching at its shoulder and pushing itself back up against the base of the tree it was resting against.

"You were about to escape," Senyara said. "I can't have that. We had a deal. You must lead me to the dragon."

The Gangraider slowly stood up.

"What's your name?" Senyara asked.

"Horritch!" it said, angrily. "My name is Horritch. What's *yours*!?"

Senyara knew it didn't really care what her name was. "Senyara," she said. "My name is Senyara."

"Well, Senyara, look over there!" the Gangraider pointed to its left, and Senyara looked. Now there was a clearing amongst the trees, and beyond it was a valley. The valley of grass and flowers led to a tall dark hill on the other side, where the sky began to turn from blue to dark and grey.

"Hades lives there. Under that hill. That's where all of his treasure is," Horritch said, still clutching the back of his shoulder. "Can I go now?"

"How do I know you are telling me the truth?" Senyara said. "That could be any old hill. You need to prove to me that is really where Hades lives."

"How?" Horritch hissed, wondering how the dark grey sky above the hill was not proof enough.

"Come with me," Senyara said, grabbing Horritch's ear again.

*

Back at the village, Senyara's father had been reading the note Senyara had left him on his bed. The note read:

Dear Father,

I know we will not have enough food to last through the winter. I have seen the monster eating everything. I have gone to find some treasure, and I will be back soon.

Senyara.

Senyara's father, whose name was Gorjin, dropped the note back on the bed.

He fell to his knees, looked up at the ceiling of his cabin and said:

"Please do not take her to Hades the dragon."

*

"Hades the dragon will eat us alive," Horritch said as he walked slightly behind Senyara, down a slope and into the valley that led to the dark hill in the distance.

"He won't," Senyara said. "He won't see us. I can move very quietly. And I won't take you so close to put you in danger. I'll let you go free."

161

For a moment, Horritch's hard mind softened. No one had ever showed him even the slightest bit of compassion before.

"Why not?" Horritch said. "My people put you in this position. Why wouldn't you want to see me eaten alive?"

"I'm not sure," Senyara said. "Maybe it would be best if you were eaten up, but for some reason, I think you should live. I don't know why. Maybe there's some good in you."

Horritch went quiet for the rest of the journey. He felt something strange inside of him, something warm, and it was directed in Senyara's direction. He didn't know what it was, but he did know that for the first time in his life, it didn't feel like such a burden and a strain to be alive. Even walking towards what he was convinced might be his impending doom, he had a slight spring in his step.

"There's a secret entrance," Horritch said. "I wasn't going to tell you about it, but if you really want to go undetected, I'll show you where it is."

"Okay," Senyara said. "Thank you. I just need enough treasure to buy food for the winter with. How much do you think I'll need?"

"The red gemstones are the most valuable," Horritch said. "You'll only need one of those. Each one is worth about ten fat bags of gold. Big bags. Bigger than me. But those red gemstones are rare. They are about the size of your fist, and when you touch them, they glow slightly."

Senyara kept the image of a red gemstone in her mind, and she felt it in her hand, as if she already had it. Then, as she looked ahead in the distance, she saw four men on horseback, and they were riding towards them across the dark valley. Horritch was still clutching occasionally at the wound on his shoulder, but it had stopped bleeding. Gangraiders' bodies were particularly tough and durable, and the pain was beginning to leave him.

"Those men will try to rob us," Horritch said. "I can feel it already."

"Well, we have nothing on us," Senyara said.

"Your weapons," Horritch said. "They will want your weapons. Your daggers. Your sword. "

Senyara kept walking as the men on large horses drew closer to them. She could feel the grass and ground of the valley beneath her feet begin to rumble as the horses galloped, and she heard one of the horses sniff and snort as they began to slow down.

"Stop!" one of the men said to Senyara. "Stop right there!"

Senyara kept moving forward.

"Stop!" one of the men yelled, and as the horses they were on skidded to a halt in front of Horritch and Senyara, Senyara noticed that these men were finely clothed.

"Where are you two going?" one of the men in the middle said. He was handsome, with a big brown beard and long brown hair. His clothes looked like they were made of silk, and over the top was a loose iron mesh that was clearly some kind of armour.

"Never you mind!" Horritch said. "Our business is our own!"

Horritch snarled at the men and the one in the middle smiled.

"You look lost," the man said. Their horses parted ways as Senyara walked through them. Then she realised she did not want to be surrounded, or attacked from behind, so she stopped, turned and faced them. She let Horritch's ear go, and he shook his arms out, as if he was ready to fight.

"We are fine," Senyara said. "What do you want with us? Are you trying to rob us?"

The handsome man in the middle laughed again. "Rob you? A young girl and a little beast? No of course not! But we are concerned to see you alone here. Do you know where you are headed?"

"In the direction of Hades the dragon," Senyara said. "We know."

The men all seemed to freeze on top of their horses.

"You don't...you don't plan to steal from the dragon, do you?" the handsome man said.

Senyara paused.

"Why?" she said. "What's it to you?"

"Because if you know how to sneak up on the dragon...if you know how to access his lair in a way he will not detect, then we want in. We want our riches back that Hades stole from our village ten years ago. We were only younglings then. But now we are men. Men who want to kill that dragon and take everything he has."

"We don't want to kill it," Senyara said. "I just want to take enough treasure to buy food for the winter."

"If you let us help you," the handsome man on horseback said, "then you will have enough to buy food and anything else you want for an entire lifetime. We can carry plenty away with our bags on horseback." The man pointed to the bags hanging off the side of all the horses.

Senyara was unsure. She didn't even feel comfortable stealing a little piece of treasure from the dragon, but she thought she had no choice.

"No," Senyara said. "No, we are going alone."

Senyara began to back away.

"Young girl," the man on horseback said, jumping down and approaching her. As soon as he got close, Horritch lunged for the man's arms with bare fangs so sharp that they would have cut straight through his loose armour.

The man lurched backwards, surprised that this little grey monster could move with such speed and ferocity.

"I'm sorry," Senyara said, "but I don't want to kill the dragon or take everything from it. I just need a little bit of treasure for my own people. I'm sorry."

Senyara turned and ran. The handsome man and his friends began to back away as they saw little Horritch snarling at them, ready to fight to the death for this little girl who had showed him a glimpse of mercy. Then Horritch turned and ran away too, and he followed Senyara to the base of the dark cloud-covered hill in the distance.

*

"I'm sorry," Horritch said, as he and Senyara reached the base of the hill. It was now cold, the clouds overhead were making it so dark that Senyara could barely see the grey body of Horritch to the left of her.

"Sorry for what?" she said.

"I'm sorry for what we did to you and your village, sending the Cropmuncher in to distract you all, trying to loot your village for treasure, I didn't know..."

"What?" Senyara said, looking around at the dark trees either side at the base of the hill.

"I didn't realise a human being could be like you. We were always told that humans were the enemy, terrible creatures who killed anything that got in their way. That's why we never had a problem stealing from them. But maybe we were told wrong."

Senyara looked at the dark figure of the little Gangraider, who was staring at her with big, sorrowful eyes.

"Some humans might be like that," Senyara said. "But my people aren't. We are good. We only fight if we have to."

"Senyara," Horritch said, lowering himself to one knee and looking at the ground. "I am now at your service. I will help you get what you need so that you can provide for your people."

"You already *are* helping," Senyara said, finding it astonishing how this little vicious creature had changed so drastically just because she said she wouldn't feed him to the dragon. "You already helped keep me safe from those men. Thank you. Now how do we get into this mountain?"

"There are two entrances," Horritch said, standing to his feet. "The first is commonly known, perhaps already known by those men back there, but it is dangerous. Creatures do not use it unless they believe Hades is distracted. The second entrance is far more stealthy, not known by many creatures at all. A Gangraider used the second entrance once, years ago...but Senyara...even though the entrance is sneaky...that Gangraider never came back. We never saw him again. We think he was eaten by Hades."

"Or..." Senyara said, "he got so much treasure for himself that he went away and started a new life. Show me the entrance, now, please. I don't want the men to chase us down and see where we go."

"Ok!" Horritch said, beginning to sprint directly up the side of the hill. "This way!"

*

"Just follow me," Horritch said to Senyara as he sprinted up the hill ahead of her. "Just do exactly as I do..."

Just as Horritch said those last few words, he disappeared down into the side of the hill. It was as if the ground had decided to swallow him up, and all Senyara saw was his big grey hands with sharp nails flailing in the air as his body was sucked down into the ground.

Senyara stopped. She turned around. In the distance, in the valley, she could see the four men on horseback, staring at her. Then as she turned to face the hill again, she saw the grey, wiry hand of Horritch reach up out of the ground and snatch her down into the earth.

It went dark all of a sudden, and now Senyara was standing beside Horritch, in darkness, in the side of the hill.

"Be quiet," Horritch said to her. "This is usually a trap of Hades, according to old stories. A creature will fall down here and begin to call out for help. Then Hades will come along, remove the trap door beneath us and eat it."

Senyara looked around her but it was dark everywhere. She didn't know if she was surrounded by walls or by space.

"Come," Horritch whispered. "You follow me." Horritch took Senyara by the hand, wrapping his fingers tightly around her wrist, and he led her away through dark corridors where the earth was spongy beneath her feet.

Soon in the distance she could see a golden, glowing light. Horritch stopped.

"The treasure lies before us," Horritch said. "And the dragon too." He crept, now more slowly, still leading Senyara behind him, until the golden light became so bright ahead of them that Senyara began to squint. Together they reached a stony ledge, peered over the side, and looked down to see an ocean of gold coins, rubies and treasure, with a large dark red dragon sleeping in the middle of it.

"That's Hades," Horritch whispered. "We have to climb down this wall, find a red gemstone and get out of here without waking him up. If he wakes, he will probably burn us alive."

Senyara now felt the insides of her body beginning to tremble. She could hear the dragon's breathing below them. The air was unusually warm. She felt trapped underground and wasn't sure if she should risk everything for the sake of some treasure. But before she could reconsider, Horritch had released her wrist, and he was climbing down over the side of the ledge, into the treasure below.

"No!" Senyara hissed as quietly as she could. "Horritch!"

Horritch looked up at her and winked one of his big eyes, and he continued to climb down to the treasure. Senyara stood and watched, too afraid to climb down herself. If the dragon opened its eyes, that would be the end, but she felt torn and compelled to help little Horritch, who had now reached the treasure below and was gently creeping over the gold coins, heading for a big red gemstone that was sticking out to the left of the dragon.

The dragon's breathing sounded as if the air was being punched every few seconds. Horritch was trying to stay low to the ground, but as he moved in line with the nostrils of the dragon, he stumbled slightly. The force of the dragon's breath started to move him from side to side, and he stumbled, Senyara watched the dragon's eyes for any sign of movement. Its scales were sharp and its wings folded on its back had huge talons sticking out of the top. She wanted to scream to Horritch to just come back, but she couldn't, in case she woke the dragon.

And then, just as Horritch moved past the nostrils of Hades, Senyara saw the dragon sniff.

"It can smell him!" she said to herself. "Surely it can smell him!"

But the dragon did not wake up. It kept sleeping, and Horritch clearly became excited as he drew closer to the red gemstone ahead of him, because he began to speed up. He hurried, he rushed, and as he did, he fell and stumbled onto his face, picked up the gemstone in his hands, and it began to glow.

Then Senyara saw the eyelids of the dragon open. It quickly sprung up to its feet, flared its wings, and looked down at Horritch.

"THIEF!" Hades the dragon yelled and boomed. Senyara flinched and covered her ears for a moment because the yell was so loud. The entire inside of the hill and the air around her seemed to shake.

"THIEF!" Hades yelled again, and as Senyara began to climb down the ledge to try to distract the dragon, it breathed out such hot fire over Horritch that Senyara felt her own skin begin to cook. The inside of the cave under the hill became so hot that Senyara began to think of her father back home, and the fact that she would never get to see him again.

Senyara fell into the gold coins and looked at the dragon, whose fire was white with heat, and as its breathing ceased and the torching, blazing sound that came with the flames fell quiet, Senyara looked and saw Horritch, still standing there, holding this glowing red ruby in his hands.

"No!" Hades yelled. "You have the protective gem! I did not know that it was here all along! That looks like a normal gemstone! I have feared the day that the protective gem would find its way into the hands of a thief, but I never knew it was already in my possession! Give it back. Now!"

Hades lifted his right wing and swung the huge claw on its end towards Horritch. Horritch flinched, held the gemstone tight and didn't move. As soon as the claw got near him, a red orb of light surrounded Horritch, and Hades's wing was forced to bounce off.

"No!" Hades yelled, infuriated. "Release that, now!"

Hades breathed fire on Horritch again, in frustration, but Horritch had realised what was going on. He too had heard of the protective gem, but he thought it was just a story to keep the hope of men alive who had been robbed by a dragon in their past. He never knew it was real, but he had always dreamed of what it would be like to own one himself.

Horritch began to run back towards the ledge. He placed the gemstone under one arm and held it tight, and Senyara ran towards the ledge too.

Just as Hades's fire breath ceased again, Horritch threw the gem to Senyara.

173

"Here," he said. "Place it in your shirt!"

Senyara's shirt was tucked into her trousers, and she placed the gem inside her shirt, against her skin, and then, all of a sudden, it was as if her entire world was transformed. Everything went red in her vision, and she could feel an immense, fiery power welling up within her chest.

"Not another thief!" Hades yelled, and as Senyara turned and faced him, and Hades gathered another breath of fire in his lungs, Senyara put her hands out, and she imagined water being poured over the dragon's lungs, and no more fire coming out.

Suddenly smoke began to leave Hades's dark nostrils, and the slanted eyes in the side of his head began to flinch. He coughed, and he coughed out so much smoke that the air around him became grey and cloudy.

"No! Do not leave this place. It is wrong to steal!" Hades yelled.

"But you do it!" Horritch yelled. "You have made a life out of stealing! This is how it feels!"

Senyara bent down and began to pile gold coins into her shirt.

"Senyara!" Horritch yelled, looking down at her. "Only what you can carry. Ten coins will be enough for your winter, for all your people. We must go! We do not want the dragon to figure out how to overcome the protective gem. We cannot hold on to the gem for too long!"

The dragon was still coughing, and soon Senyara began to have strange thoughts. Now she wanted *all* of this treasure. Now she wanted to replace Hades. She wanted to be the one to live here, to sleep and rest on this treasure forever and punish everyone who came close.

"We must hurry!" Horritch said. "The gem will take you over if you keep it on you for too long. I could feel it happening to me. Come. We must go!"

Senyara was now experiencing the mind of Hades as if it was her own. She wanted this treasure all for herself, and she didn't want anyone else to have it. She stuffed as many gold coins as she could in her shirt, and as she turned to reach up to the ledge behind her to climb to the top, her shirt was now so full with coins that the bottom untucked itself from her trousers, and the protective gem fell out.

Suddenly she was clear again. Her mind was her own. But she had no power. Hades would breathe fire over them again if she didn't grab the gem...

"Just the gem and ten coins!" Horritch yelled. He was now at the top of the rocky legde, looking down at her. "Be strong, Senyara!"

Senyara took the gem and threw it up to Horritch. He caught it. She took two big handfuls of gold coins, stuffed them in her pockets and began to climb up the ledge.

The dragon had stopped coughing, and just as Senyara reached the top of the ledge where Horritch was waiting, Horritch held the gemstone against her neck, and Senyara felt another claw of Hades bounce off her back. She climbed up into the dark corridor above, and together the two of them ran.

More flames surrounded them, illuminating the corridors ahead of them. Horritch took a sharp turn to the right, not going back the way they came, and as they ran, the two companions both held the gemstone together for protection.

"We must find the other exit!" Horritch said. "Hades can access the first one, as if we were his trapped prey!"

Horritch and Senyara ran, and again, Senyara had a terrible desire to turn back and fight the dragon, to steal all of his treasure.

"I want all of the dragon's treasure too!" Horritch yelled. "We have to let this gemstone go or we will be doomed to fight, and if we fight, eventually we will lose!"

"No we won't," Senyara said, stopping and grabbing Horritch by the wrist. They could hear Hades screaming and stomping inside the cave behind them. He was moving to somewhere else.

"Escaping through the secret entrance, are you!" Hades yelled, assuming they were going to the other exit. "Well you will be my prey!"

"We will lose if we stay!" Horritch said. Senyara's vision was now all red again. "The gemstone protects, but it also destroys! It uses power from the nearest dragon to protect the holder, but if held for too long – *you* also become a possession of the dragon. The dragon's power will take you over if you hold the stone for too long!"

Senyara was standing, trying to fight the desire to go back and claim all the treasure as her own. Horritch continued:

"The stone is loyal to those who seek justice, but not to those who seek to own the treasure of entire nations of people. It corrupts those who hold it for themselves for too long. You have your gold coins. You will have food for the winter, we don't need the gemstone now. The exit is close."

Horritch, with his intense new loyalty towards Senyara, managed to free himself and let the gemstone go. And as soon as he did, all of its power flooded into Senyara, and she felt completely invincible.

"I can beat that dragon," she said. "And I will!"

*

Senyara had turned around, and she was running back towards the treasure, still holding the glowing red protective gemstone. Time seemed to move very slowly for her. She felt a sudden chill in the air, and she lost all awareness of time as she continued to run.

"Stop!" Horritch yelled. "The stone will betray you if you give in to the thoughts of a dragon! That is the test! You must not become the dragon that you now have power over. If you do, you will become the dragon's victim!"

Senyara could barely hear Horritch, and she didn't even care what he had to say. If she had all of that treasure, she would be happy and safe forever. She could feel it. It was so close, and now that she could exert her power over Hades, the treasure would soon be hers.

But then, just as she was at her most excited, she felt something pierce through her ankle. She stumbled and fell, just like Horritch had stumbled and fell onto the stone amongst the treasure. She dropped the stone, hit her face on the rocky ground beneath her, and as the red, glowing gemstone skipped ahead of her body, the large boots of a man ran and stepped over her. Then another one. Then another. Then a final man ran past.

She watched as that handsome man on horseback that she had met in the valley reached down amongst his friends, picked up the stone, and suddenly his entire body began to turn red.

He looked back at Senyara, and suddenly she had clarity again. She had two pocketfuls of gold coins. She had enough.

"Thank you, young girl," the man said, with his friends by his side. He could feel what this gemstone was. He had heard about the protective gem of power, and since his vision had turned red, he knew he was holding it in his hands. "You and that little wretch distracted the dragon for us. And now, with this power, we will take the dragon for everything he has."

The men all turned and ran away down the dark stony corridor, yelling and screaming like warriors, and Senyara felt something pick her up beneath her body.

"Come, Senyara, we must leave quickly," Horritch said, carrying her on his back.

"Horritch?" Senyara said, feeling the searing pain in the bottom of her leg where an arrow was still sticking out. "You said you would protect me."

"I did," Horritch said, "I told that man I would eat him if he did you any permanent harm, so he aimed for your leg. And now you are safe."

Just as Horritch reached the end of the corridor, he turned, and soon he saw an open doorway that led to the forest outside.

"Opening this door makes the inside of Hades's cave very cold," Horritch said. "It is well-known know that opening it will cause Hades to wake and breathe fire through the tunnels to stop intruders. But the men knew that he was distracted."

Horritch carried Senyara through the open door into the forest outside, and he began to carry her back towards the valley behind the mountain.

"There is a man ahead of us," Horritch said. "He is running towards us."

Senyara turned, looked over the front of Horritch's shoulder and said:

"Yes. That's my father."

*

180

It didn't take long before Senyara's father, Gorjin, reached the two of them, while Horritch was still carrying Senyara over his shoulder.

"What are you doing?!" Senyara's father yelled as he ran up to Horritch, drawing a sword from his waist and ready to cut Horritch in half.

Horritch quickly put Senyara down and stepped back.

"It's okay," Senyara said, raising her hands up towards her father to stop him from attacking. "He saved me!"

"That's a Gangraider, Senyara!"

"Yes, he's different," Senyara said, still holding up her hands. "Don't hurt him."

Senyara's father stopped, kneeled down and looked at the arrow in Senyara's lower leg.

"We must take you to the Healing Lake," he said. "Let's go, quickly."

Senyara's father picked her up over his own shoulder, carried her away, and Horritch followed behind, keeping his distance.

As Senyara's father made his way down into the valley, Senyara felt a strong fear begin to bubble underneath her skin.

"Father," she said. "I feel as if something is about to happen. Something bad."

Suddenly all three of them heard a tremendous roar come from inside the hill where Hades lived, and the battle cries of four men who were now assailing the dragon. Senyara began to look around. She wondered if other dragons would come to help Hades, if they could sense he was in danger.

Senyara's father continued to walk forward, but as he did, Senyara looked up and saw in the sky above the figure of something large and dark.

"Is that...is that a bird up there?" she said. Senyara's father briefly looked up, but could not see the shape directly above him.

"Never mind about birds," he said. "Let us get you to the Healing Lake. Are you sure that Gangraider behind us is safe? I don't trust it."

"Yes. He saved my life," Senyara said. "But father, up there, that bird is becoming larger..."

"Dragon!" Horritch yelled from behind them. "Dragon above! Run!"

Now Senyara could see the flying wide-winged figure in the sky above them turning downwards, pulling its wings back and beginning to dive down towards them.

"Run! Run!" Horritch yelled again, and as the figure in the sky grew quickly larger, Horritch could see it was a large grey dragon, the size of a big tree. It was headed directly towards them.

Senyara's father ran, but he had not yet made it into the forest ahead of them, and as Senyara looked behind her, she saw Horritch stop.

Horritch looked at her. He waved.

"Goodbye," Horritch said to her. "You must make it to safety. The dragon will not chase you once you are in the trees. It is headed for the hill to help Hades."

And then, with Horritch as a distraction, and Senyara and her father not yet inside the safety of the forest, the grey dragon crashed into the ground ahead of Horritch, and immediately breathed fire all over him.

"No!" Senyara yelled. "No! We have to help him!"

"You heard him!" Senyara's father said. "We have to get you to safety."

And then Senyara saw something very strange. As the flames from the dragon ceased, she could see that Horritch's skin had turned black from being burnt, his body was smoking, but he was still alive. He was climbing up the dragon's leg, climbing onto its back and biting it behind its neck.

"Horritch!" Senyara yelled. "Run!"

"Off! Off me!" she heard the dragon shout. "I have heard my brother Hades calling with his thoughts, and you are the thief!"

Horritch kept clinging on and biting the dragon, and the dragon's arms were too short to reach back and pull him away.

As Senyara's father managed to enter into the forest, all he could see was Horritch still on the dragon's back, and as a tree blocked her view, she was sure she saw the dragon stumble.

"The dragons will always remember you now," Senyara's father said to her. "They share one mind. They will have all seen your face. You will now be known to them as a dragon thief, and it would not be safe for you to ever be close to one again, even if you do not intend to steal."

"Okay," Senyara said, feeling her heart so heavy after watching Horritch sacrifice himself for her. "Okay."

*

After a while of running through the trees with his daughter still being carried over his shoulders, Senyara's father made it to a small pool of water, that was known to his people as 'The Healing Lake'.

Instantly he threw his daughter in. She disappeared for a moment, submerged under the water, and then her head burst above the surface and she yelled:

"Why did you do that! Only my leg was hurt!"

"The whole body is connected," Senyara's father said. "And you might have been carrying an injury that you weren't aware of. We have to be sure."

Senyara climbed out of the pool herself, and as she stood up, dripping wet and looking around at the circle of trees around them, she glanced down to her leg, and saw that the arrow had disappeared. She reached down, touched her leg above her ankle and there was no sign of injury.

"Wow," she said. "But you should have warned me before you threw me in, though, father, I could have lost *these*..."

Senyara reached inside her pockets and took out the two handfuls of golds coins that were wedged deep inside. As she showed them to her father, his face turned aghast, as if she was holding poison.

"Is that dragon's gold?" he hissed. "You actually stole from a dragon?"

Senyara's heart sank. Not only was Horritch probably dead, but now it seemed he had died in vain.

"You can use it," she said. "You can use it to buy food."

"I plan to visit the Replicator to take care of our food needs!" Senyara's father snapped. "We have enough left to salvage, to ask the Replicator to create more of. You were foolish to steal a dragon's gold. A dragon thief forever carries a scent that all other dragons can smell. Even the Healing Lake will not be able to wash it off, and we have been warned that spending dragon's gold can lead to misfortune."

"Maybe that's just what the dragons want us to think," Senyara said.

"Well I am not willing to risk it," her father said. "That gold is useless to us."

Senyara looked at the shining gold coins in her wet hands, and her eyes began to fill with tears. It had all been for nothing.

"Will you not use the gold for anything? Can't we pay the Replicator?"

"No!" Senyara's father said, angrily. "No. You have risked your life for nothing. You should have told me before you left! The Replicator does not take gold as payment. It asks for something else..."

Through her still teary eyes, Senyara looked beyond her father to the forest behind him, and she saw a small, dark, smoking figure staggering through the trees.

"Senyara!" a raspy voice called. "Senyara! "

"Horritch!" Senyara yelled. "Horritch! Come here, jump in this pool!"

Senyara dropped her gold coins on the ground and ran over to Horritch.

"Don't touch me!" he said, raising his arms. "I feel as if I might fall apart."

Senyara could see all of Horritch's skin had turned flaky and charred, as if he was made of paper that had been burnt to ashes. He slowly staggered past her, with his face wincing but his eyes still bright in his burnt and blackened face, and as he made it to the edge of the Healing Lake, he fell into the water.

Senyara watched at the water's edge, with her father behind her. For a moment the crystal-clear water turned black, and as it turned clear again, Horritch's head rose above the water, and he looked up and smiled at her with the same viciously sharp teeth.

"Better," he said. "I'm all better."

*

187

"I don't know what happened," Horritch said a few minutes later, after he had climbed out of the Healing Lake. He was now sitting at its edge with his feet resting inside the water. "I think it was from holding that protective gemstone. I still had power in me. The dragon's flames hurt, they burnt, but they didn't kill me. I was able to fight it, and I fought it for long enough that it decided to try to get away from me, and it headed for the hill to help Hades fight those thieving men."

Senyara's father was still standing, and Senyara had sat down beside her friend, Horritch.

"Thank you," she said to Horritch, putting her arm around his bony shoulder, whose skin now looked clean and fresh. "You saved me. You saved me twice."

Horritch stood and turned to Senyara's father.

"I'm sorry for what my people did to you," Horritch said to the big man. "I have one more debt to pay. I heard you saying you are going to see the Replicator. I know that the Replicator demands at least five years of a person's life for it to replenish food stores. I would like to donate mine, as an apology for what me and the other Gangraiders did to your village.

Senyara's father stood and bowed at Horritch, and Horritch bowed back.

"No," Senyara said. "Isn't there another way?"

Horritch looked down beside Senyara and saw the gold coins on the ground.

"And then," Horritch said, "I will donate more of my years so that the Replicator replicates those gold coins. Then we can share them. There will be enough to convince the other Gangraiders that we no longer need to raid and steal. Our worries will be over. No Gangraider has ever wanted to take years off their own lives in order to make the lives of others better. But now, after fighting alongside Senyara, I feel it is my purpose. But you must show me the way, large man. I do not know how to find the Replicator."

Senyara stood up and looked at her father.

"Thank you," he said. "I will show you the way."

And now, with Senyara and Horritch holding hands, Horritch knelt down to the ground and scooped up all the gold coins so that they were enclosed in his long grey fingers, and together the three of them walked off, to find the Replicator.

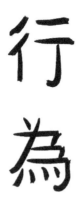

Deed

A good deed done without expectation of reward, often brings unexpected benefits.

The Protective Gems Of Power

There are only three of these gems known to exist in this world. One guards against dragons, another guards against humans, and the other guards against the beasts of the forest. If anyone brings all three together, the gems are said to form a necklace that will protect the wearer against anything in this world.

The Ninja Chronicles – Part 2
Coming Soon!

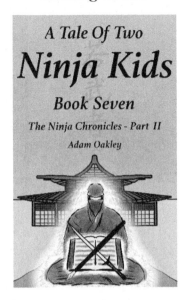

Join the Forbidden Ninja, Dengor The Great, Hirozama and Senyara as they continue their quests to overcome evil and discover their true powers, along with more stories of ancient ninjas and warriors who used their skills to accomplish great things.

Follow on social media to find out about the launch of Book 8:

@NinjaKidsBook

www.NinjaKidsBook.com

"Henrik The Defender"

- OUT NOW ON AMAZON! -

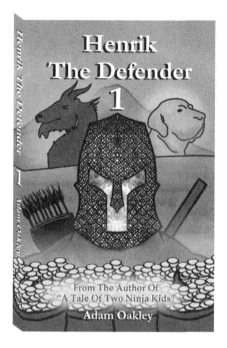

Discover more of Henrik's adventures as he moves into adulthood and his fighting skills are put to the test.

Join Henrik and his loyal Fighting Hound named Boevill as they work together to protect the Kingdom of Argad from an evil force, alongside some of the magical fighting creatures from Henrik's past...

Get the book now on Amazon!

"Fred: The Creature Sent To Save Us All"

- OUT NOW ON AMAZON! -

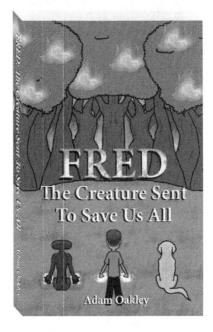

You have met Fred at the end of "A Tale Of Two Ninja Kids - Book 6", and now you can join his adventures with Wallace as he tries to save the Chatamanga Rainforest from destruction, uncovering a strange new world that Wallace never expected...

10% of profits will be used to plant new trees.

Get the book now on Amazon!

"Mythical Creatures Of The Forest"

- OUT NOW ON AMAZON! -

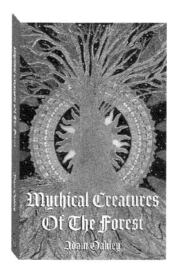

Discover more stories about the Garganfan, the Mountain Man, and learn about when Amanda and Greg first discovered the magic of the forest.

Meet the Dundenbeast, the Shapeshifter, Heelog, the Treekeeper, the Feasting Tree, the Pikaloo, the Healybug and many others...

Join Dr Bernard J. Hoothfellow as he embarks on his mission to discover all the creatures in the forest that no one believes to be real.

Adventure awaits.

Get the book now on Amazon!

"Happiness Is Inside: 25 Inspirational Stories For Greater Peace Of Mind"

- OUT NOW ON AMAZON! -

Inspirational short stories for ages 8 and up...

Meet the boy who could not worry, the man who has become free from labels, the mysterious bear who has wisdom to share, and the frog who has discovered the secret to lasting joy.

These are great stories for parents and children to read together or alone, and each have their own message for a more fulfilling life.

Get the book now on Amazon!

Audiobooks

Audiobooks available on Amazon, Audible, Apple and AdamOakleyBooks.com

Book Reviews

ENJOYING THE SERIES?

PLEASE LEAVE SOME GOOD REVIEWS ON AMAZON TO HELP THE BOOKS REACH YOUNG NINJAS EVERYWHERE!

THANK YOU!

About The Author

Adam is an author from the UK who loves to write all different kinds of books.

He writes books about inner peace, inner power, and loves writing stories that feel like stepping into other realms.

He spends his time writing, doing martial arts, growing organic food and spending time with his family.

He hopes you loved reading the book, and he is grateful for any young readers or parents who can leave a review on Amazon to help the book reach more people.

He thanks you for your support, and is always available to contact via one of his websites:

www.InnerPeaceNow.com

www.AdamOakleyBooks.com

Made in the USA
Columbia, SC
18 June 2022